MISTLETOE MEDICINE

Ever since he wrecked her romance with Dr Dickie Derby, Nurse Hannah Westcott has harboured a thorough dislike of Dr Jonathan Boyd-Harrington — but she never expected to see him again. To her horror, he turns up as Senior Registrar at the Royal Hanoverian Hospital, and there is no way she can avoid him — especially when he takes an interest in the hospital panto. Hannah has the star part, but it would seem she must play Nurse Beauty to Jonathan Boyd-Harrington's Dr Beast . . .

ANNA RAMSAY

MISTLETOE MEDICINE

Complete and Unabridged

LINFORD
Leicester

First published in Great Britain in 1986 by
Mills & Boon Limited
London

First Linford Edition
published 2013
by arrangement with
Mills & Boon Limited
London

A catalogue record for this book is available
from the British Library.

ISBN 978–1–4448–1795–9

Published by
F. A. Thorpe (Publishing)
Anstey, Leicestershire

Set by Words & Graphics Ltd.
Anstey, Leicestershire
Printed and bound in Great Britain by
T. J. International Ltd., Padstow, Cornwall

This book is printed on acid-free paper

1

'Hannah in paradise!'

'What was that?' demanded Dr Richard Derby, bestriding Hannah's prone form and flicking her with drops of water as he roughly towelled his handsome, dripping head. He rested a damp foot none too lightly on her bare stomach. 'What did you say?'

Hannah just smiled like the Mona Lisa, squinting adoringly up at Dickie, who stood framed like a dark satyr against the fierce gold sun. Of course it was like being in paradise! Her first ever trip abroad. Invited to spend the whole of August in the south of France, guest of her best friend's parents, in a farmhouse set deep among the herb-scented hills of Provence.

Paradise to be driven down in Mr Fitzpatrick's swish white Roller — as his daughter so irreverently described that sumptuous car. And paradise to have darling Dickie, Hannah's doctor boyfriend, summoned to join them for five whole glorious days.

'Mmmm . . . ' sighed the ecstatic girl, stretching out her slim golden limbs in sun worship, 'so this is how the other half lives. I'll work on my tan for just five more minutes, then do six lengths of the pool. D'you know, Dickie, this place is lovelier than my wildest dreams . . . *magical*. Don't you think France is *the* most romantic country . . . mmm, darling?'

But Dr Richard Derby had wandered off in search of another drink.

Hannah closed her eyes again and let her thoughts just drift with the haze of heat. Mango's parents were being unbelievably kind and generous to her. They really seemed to approve of the girls' friendship. Mr Fitzpatrick had said Hannah was like another daughter to him, and what a good influence she was on the wayward, exotic Mona-Geraldine. It made Hannah blush with embarrassment, and of course it wasn't true. She was the grateful one.

'This is a reward for you both,' Graeme Fitzpatrick had insisted. 'You've put in eighteen months of hard work and gained your orthopaedic certificates. Have a really good holiday before you start your SRN training in London. I'm proud to have a daughter who wants to earn her own living instead of going in for the debby life. Bring your boy-friends, invite anyone you like. Enjoy yourselves.'

'Look, Dad, we haven't enough bedrooms for all my Oxford boy-friends!' declared Mango with a wink at her friend. 'Hannah's the one with the faithful nature. She's been dating our hospital heart-throb for nearly a year now. If he's got some leave stored up, I dare say we could twist Dr Derby's arm to join us. As for me, I'm going to sample the local talent.'

Her father had whacked her affec-tionately about her curly head with a rolled-up copy of the *Financial Times*, but left the girls to make their own arrangements. A wealthy City stockbroker, he was preoccupied with weightier issues.

And Hannah's mind was preoccupied with the knowledge that while she would now be nursing in London, at the orthopaedic hospital in Oxford Dickie Derby would find plenty of other girls eager to console him in off-duty hours.

She locked her hands behind her head, raising her upper body to admire Dickie as he prowled along the diving board and launched himself down into the glittering turquoise waters of the pool. His olive skin took mere hours to tan to perfection. And although he wasn't quite the six feet he might claim — his legs, criticised Mango with a giggle, were on the skinny side — the impressionable Hannah had been overwhelmed to be singled out by such a popular young houseman.

Eleven months and four days since their first date: like a schoolgirl she'd kept count of the passage of time. He'd driven her into the centre of Oxford, parked in St Giles, and she'd been so nervous and proud as they strolled through the crowds to the cinema in Walton Street. And then he'd taken her for a drink in the Randolph Hotel — and when she asked for pineapple juice he'd pretended to faint from astonishment and made her laugh so much everyone had stared. During the drive back to Headington in his battered red two-seater with its cracked draughty hood, he'd asked, 'What does your father do?'

And I said, remembered Hannah with a private grin of recollection, 'My father's the vicar of — ' And I had to make a grab for the steering wheel and stop us hitting a bus!

Still, it hadn't after all put Dr Derby off. He'd been dating her regularly ever since.

'It's so romantic here. Perhaps — ' Hannah hesitated, hardly daring to whisper her dream aloud, even for her own ears. Her thick dark lashes trembled and her hazel eyes were bright with unshed tears. She rolled over on to her front and pressed her nose into the hot, aromatic grass.

'Be sensible, Westcott!' she scolded herself. 'You're nineteen, not twenty-nine. Wait till you've got that SRN after your name. If Dickie really loves you, if it's meant to be, he'll propose marriage then. But don't suppose he won't play the field in the meantime. Come September, you'll be in London and he'll be there in Oxford — and you know him well enough to foretell what that means!'

Dickie Derby sprang out of the pool and came back to plant a foot on the small of Hannah's back and make as if to tread heavily on her vulnerable spine. 'Still dreaming you're in paradise, my little angel?' he taunted. 'If you're not in that water within ten seconds, I'll pick you up bodily and chuck you in the deep end.'

'Don't be rotten to poor Hannah!'

reproved Mango Fitzpatrick, climbing out of the pool and tugging off her bathing cap to reveal a mass of shoulder-length raven curls; five feet and nine inches of elegant white-skinned slenderness, displayed to advantage in a strapless black Fiorucci bikini of startling brevity.

Derby, you're a cad! she thought critically. You know darn well Hannah's absolutely aching inside.

'Han's one of the world's workers. Let her snooze in peace if that's what she wants.'

Pinned by his hostess's challenging eye, Dickie just smiled and acknowledged a superior will. Mango was one tough cookie and nobody's fool. He knew he was tolerated for Hannah's sake rather than for his own charm. He'd often thought it interesting that these two were such opposites, yet such close friends. Opposite in every way — looks and temperament, background and lifestyle.

Hannah was a fascinating girl, soft and warm and gentle, body and soul, yet passionate and tempestuous when roused. She'd take on anyone for a good cause: it was one of her themes, the equality of man. Her vicarage upbringing, Dickie guessed. All men equal in the eyes of God, wasn't that the usual sermon? One of her special beefs was the arrogance of some of the medical profession. She'd better watch her step at the Royal Hanoverian, bastion of pomp and renown.

Great time we had together, mused Dickie, glancing at his watch before fixing himself another Pernod with water and ice. Happy memories.

★   ★   ★

It was late afternoon when their peace was shattered by the roar of a car's exhaust, amplified by enclosing court-yard walls, and the imperious summons of a car horn.

'Who the devil can that be?' exclaimed Mango impatiently. Her parents had driven to Paris for a couple of nights, and she was not in the mood for acting polite hostess to unexpected callers. 'Come on, you two, try and look like a crowd so they think they're interrupting a party. Ouch! These stone flags are hot!'

She led the way, padding barefoot round the terrace and ducking under the rose-laden archway leading into the courtyard beyond, Dickie sauntering at her heels in his red bathing slip and Hannah dutifully making up the rear.

A silver streak of expensive open-topped machinery was drawn up on sunbaked cobbles worn smooth with age. Leaning against the bonnet with bored expression and arms folded was the driver; his companion standing motionless, head tilted back and hands cupped to shield his eyes as he examined the meticulously restored Provençal farmhouse with its golden-tiled rooftops and vine-clad walls.

Hannah saw two men — confident in bearing, arrogant in manner — and clearly rather rich, if their transport was anything to go by. Stripped to the waist

9

and displaying strongly muscled bodies in beige Bermuda shorts. She was especially startled to hear Dickie's roar of greeting.

'Would you ever believe it! Seb, you old son-of-a-gun, what on earth brings you here?'

But the blond man had grabbed Mango's scantily clad form in a bear hug of unabashed intimacy that suggested he had excellent reasons for being in that particular spot. 'Darling Mango — stunning as ever.' He released the girl and aimed a fist at Dr Derby's taut solar plexus. 'And Dickie — my old partner in crime!'

Feeling awkward in the face of this raucous camaraderie, Hannah hung back beneath the rambling primrose-scented canopy of Félicité and Perpétue roses, the sweet clusters of creamy pompons and shiny dark-green leaves forming an aureole about her curvaceous golden shape, sensuously revealed by a faded pink cotton bikini. The dark man from behind inscrutable lenses was giving Mango

10

cool appraisal; no one was aware of Hannah.

Sebastian, the blond giant, was acting exceedingly gallant. From a sun-bleached terracotta urn planted with lilies a little past their best, he had plucked a waxen flower which he was tucking among the luxuriant raven curls behind Mango's left ear. Big brother wasn't making much effort, observed Hannah from her place in the shadows. He gave the impression that Sebastian's behaviour was rather juvenile and that Mona-Geraldine Fitzpatrick was just another stupid and empty-headed play-girl. *He* hadn't been the one to decide to make this unexpected visit, guessed Hannah with a wry lift of her brow.

Suddenly her own interest was sharpened by the realisation that these two men were brothers and doctors, therefore not the idle playboys she had mistaken them for. Her alert eyes travelled from the group of three across to where the sombre man still lounged against the long silver bonnet of his pantherlike sports car. That monster hadn't come cheap, she mused. On a medic's pay? He must be one of those wealthy Harley Street men. But surely a bit on the young side . . .

When a pair of unsmiling, hooded eyes trapped her own, Hannah almost jumped out of her skin. He'd whipped away the sunglasses, revealing the direction of his gaze. Caught her boldly in the act of rudely staring.

Five yards or so separated them. But the blood rose in her cheeks and she dropped her eyelids in silly girlish embarrassment. 'For goodness' sake!' she muttered in stinging self-reproof, 'since when does a Westcott blush?' Defiance flickered in the hazel eyes that tangled now with the glinting regard of the silent stranger.

'Can't get over it, Derby, finding *you* here of all places,' Sebastian was exclaiming with a discreet wink that Hannah did not miss in her secret corner. For a fleeting moment she wondered . . . but Seb's next words had her biting her lip.

'So our delicious Mango has succumbed to your fatal charm. Jon! Get your moody presence over here. You told me you hadn't seen this vision since she was about ten. And you must remember Dickie Derby — the guy who shared my flat in medical school. You know, the one who pulled more birds than — '

Mango interrupted with a hasty shriek, 'Dickie's not *my* boyfriend, you idiot! He's staying here with my friend Hannah. Hannah, stop pretending you're one of those church-mouse sort of vicars' daughters and come on over here and introduce yourself. Shyness was never one of your more obvious assets.'

Hannah walked slowly forward on noiseless bare feet — a nymph emerging from her bower, thought the older doctor, grinning inwardly at his uncharacteristically poetic turn of phrase, only the twist of his severe mouth betraying the glimmer of interest the girl had aroused. Perfectly ordinary in the light of day. It must have been the picturesque setting she'd been hiding in. Beside that other exotic beauty, this one was more wholesome and substantial. Looked as if she'd bought the two-piece when she was a whole size smaller. Younger too than he'd suspected, in spite of the poised carriage of the head and the graceful line of neck and shoulders. But those eyes! Great long lashes hiding a touch of steel. No, she hadn't liked him staring at her as if she was horse-meat. Tough!

Everyone was regarding Hannah now as she came to join the group with head held high and a brave smile. She'd never let them guess she was overawed by the unexpected arrival of these two alarmingly confident brothers. After that awful mistake about Dickie and Mango, it was vital Dickie should not be ashamed to acknowledge what they meant to each other.

Her hair had dried in the sun till it foamed about her neck in airy bronzed tendrils. She looked extremely pretty, and a proprietorial arm reached out and drew her possessively to her lover's side. Seb grinned and turned back to the sensational Mango, all dazzling white skin and yard-long legs. 'My brother, Dr Jonathan Boyd-Harrington,' he said in formal introduction.

Mango's black eyes danced. 'Stay the night, both of you — we've masses of spare room.'

Sebastian was charmingly regretful. 'Jon's on call on Wednesday. We've been down to Antibes to drop some of Mother's stuff off at the villa — cost a bomb to send it by rail. Camilla didn't really want to be left alone this week. But Jon drives like the devil — ' Seb indicated the gleaming silver machine with a backward nod of his handsome blond head and added cheerfully, ' — so she'll soon get him back!'

No one ventured to explain about Camilla, so Hannah assumed she must be Jon's wife. Pretty spectacular Camilla must be, to have caught such a formidable eye.

'At least join us for a swim to cool off,' coaxed Mango.

Hannah followed the others as they all walked round to the gardens. *Cool off?* Dr Jon looked about as cool as you could get and still breathe. Heaven help his patients, mused Hannah with a little moue that pulled her full mouth down at the corners. He gave off no sense of personal warmth, but rather a dark brooding arrogance that could frighten you half to death if you let it get to you. He'd got nice hair, though, thick and dark and silky with just a suggestion of a wave and one untamed lock dipping over his right eyebrow. He'd look great in his white coat. And doubtless considered himself to be so. The great Dr Jonathan Boyd-Harrington.

She would keep well out of his way. The brothers would soon be gone.

★ ★ ★

The seagull flew down for a closer look at the group of English doctors and nurses sporting themselves by the swimming pool. To the bird, that shimmering

16

patch of turquoise was a sea in miniature, and it fastened upon that sea with an inquisitive beady eye.

There was a big dark man scything up and down the pool as if in training for the next Olympics, while two younger doctors, both housemen on surgical firms, were fooling about on the water's edge trying vainly to distract the attention of two pretty nurses away from the swimmer and his impressive performance.

The girls lay face down on the lawn, chins resting on folded arms as they concentrated on the Senior Registrar and exchanged whispered comments not intended for the ears of Dickie and Sebastian.

'Mean, moody . . . and quite magnificent!' pronounced Mango with satisfaction and an arch of sable eyebrows as exotic as her self-given nickname. She had been christened to please Great-Aunts Mona and Geraldine, and it didn't suit her half as aptly as Mango. She nudged her companion with a sharply elegant elbow.

'You're unusually quiet. You must be sickening for something.'

'Rubbish!' But Hannah bit her lip and avoided Mango's clever eye. To a student nurse, a Registrar was a mighty figure indeed. And if he so happened to look, heaven help him, like a hero stepped straight from the legends of Greek mythology . . . well, it added a frisson of excitement to the indubitably interesting Jonathan Boyd-Harrington.

But at the same time Hannah was considerably annoyed with herself. She was not the sort of person who set doctors upon pedestals, forgetting they were as human as any two-footed being. At least she hoped she was not so foolish! But here was someone who struck her most forcibly as a man out of the ordinary. He could be a road-sweeper and still she would feel this extraordinary physical awareness of the man himself.

In spite of the heat Hannah shivered, peering through the sweep of her eyelashes at the powerful swimmer in the pool. 'I don't like you,' she breathed into the crook of her arm. 'But I feel safer if I keep you well in focus.'

'I can see what you're up to,' teased Mango, making not the slightest attempt to disguise her own interest. 'You can't take your eyes off him either . . . in front of your darling boyfriend too, tut tut! Phew, I'm sweating like a pig. Time to slosh on more of the sunblock lotion or I'll be looking like a magnolia caught in a very nasty frost and no one will give me a second glance.'

Smitten! It was so far from the truth Hannah didn't bother to protest, knowing Mango's well-meaning intent was to divert her from feeling sad about parting from Dickie. 'Will you look at those two down in the shallow end. Do you suppose they aim to drown one another?'

'I'd rather concentrate on you know who. I remember it now — I last saw Jon when I was in Brownie uniform and he was starting medical school. Oh my, has he improved with keeping!'

Deliberately, Hannah turned her

back to gaze across the orchard to the hills beyond. 'I imagine he's accustomed to adoring glances from every female within gawping distance,' she observed drily. Built like a James Bond hero, way over the six foot mark. And that face too memorable for comfort as it loomed in her mind's eye and blotted out the vista of sky and hills. 'What happened to his nose?'

'I adore his nose. Makes him look cruel and ruthless.'

'It's been broken and badly set,' said Hannah baldly. 'And his mouth's lopsided when he attempts a smile — lack of practice!' But most of all she remembered the uncomfortable feeling produced by the four-square regard of those hawk-eyes which missed not a detail, and the highly personal intelligence which illuminated the brooding, irregular features.

Mango dabbled crimson-tipped toes in the sparkly water of the deep end. 'Big and butch and beautiful.' She gave a long sigh of pleasure. 'Just how I like my men. Unfortunately Daddy's made me swear I'll never marry a doctor. So he's all yours, Han.'

Choosing to ignore this unlooked-for generosity, Hannah hugged her knees and contemplated Mango's future. 'You'll get married as soon as you finish training,' she predicted confidently. 'You're not ambitious like me. Me, I want a blue uniform and frilly cap and a ward to call my own.'

The black-haired girl was not about to argue. Three years of making herself useful to the world at large, then yes, she hoped she'd marry a guy who'd keep her in style. 'You always were the bright one, Hannah. You really should have stayed on at your grammar school, finished those science A levels and gone in for medicine. Your mother told me the head was furious when you wouldn't consider medical school but insisted on leaving after the lower sixth to do the orthopaedic course.'

Hannah's reply was brisk and final. 'I never wanted to be a doctor. It's always been nursing for me. And it has to be the Royal Hanoverian too, following in Helen's footsteps.'

Mango stretched out her long white legs and considered whether her calves were unattractively skinny compared to Hannah's. 'Look how happy Helen is now she's married to Bram and settled in that fabulous pad in Hampstead. I suppose you could marry Dickie and still nurse.' She checked Hannah's reaction with a sidelong glance. The denial came too quick, too pat; poor Hannie must have been hoping after all.

The Westcott chin was held obstinately high. 'It's all right, Mango, I've no illusions where Dickie's concerned, never you fear. I shan't go breaking my heart for him — shan't have much time to!'

All the same Hannah glanced uncertainly in the doctors' direction: she'd just recalled Seb's wink when first he saw Dickie. Could the visit have been pre-arranged between the two of them? Had Dickie anticipated he'd be bored, after three days in her company?

'You and Sebastian seem to know each other pretty well,' she remarked with apparent nonchalance, stifling the hurtful knot twisting her heartstrings. 'How long has this been going on? I thought you were dead set on that Brookie fellow who inherited a fortune for his twenty-first.'

Mango broke into a peal of laughter. 'I'm not interested in *Seb* — not *that* way, goose!'

Oh, reflected Hannah with sinking spirits, so it *is* Dickie they've come to amuse.

'Hey, you two, come on down the shallow end and let's have a game of water polo,' suggested Dickie, sneaking up behind the two gossiping girls. 'Stop neglecting your visitors, Mango.'

'Why don't you show Seb round the place while Han and I finish our little chat . . . '

Mango knelt up, lifting the mass of raven hair off her neck in a pin-up style pose as Jonathan came storming up to the top of the pool and made a racing turn under water. 'I'm beginning to regret I ever suggested that swim!' she confided to Hannah sotto voce. 'Isn't Jon *ever* going to stop? I'd forgotten he was so fearsomely athletic, no wonder he's in such fantastic shape.' Then, recalling Hannah's tentative query, she explained, 'Our families are old friends. Seb's one of my on-and-off flames, but he knows the score, that I don't fall for doctors. Isn't he fun, though?

'Actually,' she continued slowly, wondering if she really ought to mention this to Hannah but sensing that her friend was wary of the Boyd-Harringtons, 'those brothers have rather a sad background. Their father was killed in some kind of skiing accident, but it was a most unhappy marriage and not without its effect on Jon and Seb. Lady Parry — '

'*Lady* . . . ?' echoed Hannah faintly, struggling with the stirrings of pity and curiosity which Mango's tale had aroused.

'She remarried Sir James Parry, the

diplomat — retired now. They've bought this place in Antibes. Well, as I was saying, seeing their parents so unhappy all those years when they were at an impressionable age, it's had the effect of making Big Brother cynical about marriage.'

'So he's not married,' interrupted Hannah in surprise.

'Married to medicine, my dear! Seb says no woman could compete with Jon's single-minded devotion to his work. Her life would be one of *total* neglect.'

'Well,' exclaimed Hannah, 'considering you claim not to have seen Big Brother since Brownie days, you seem to know an awful lot about his intimate feelings.'

Mango shrugged. 'Seb and I have regular heart-to-hearts when I'm in town. I'm his emotional adviser. He worries an awful about Jonathan — idolises him. Life is lonely at the top — and that's where Jon is heading.'

Surprise magnified Hannah's hazel eyes. A man like that, *lonely?* It was impossible to believe. 'What about this — er — Camilla?' she asked.

'Oh, Camilla . . . just one of the long line of professional beauties who cater for his healthy masculine appetite . . . You two idiots!' Mango suddenly shrieked. And the colour that had sprung into Hannah's cheeks went unremarked upon as both girls flung up their arms to ward off the wash as Dickie and Seb teetered crazily on the brink and toppled together into deep water, right into the swimmer's power-driving path.

'Will you take a look at that! Good thing they moved out of Mighty Man's path sharpish. He was just about to plough straight through them, the great bully!'

'Big bully,' echoed Hannah absent-mindedly. Dripping and panting, the two men dragged themselves out of the pool and relaxed beside the girls. Jon was now practising reverse dives from the springboard. They all watched the uncon-cerned display.

'Jon's pretty expert at most forms of sport,' observed Sebastian with unalloyed pride. 'You should see him on the ski slopes. If he'd only take more time off from work and give himself a break. You know my brother's a physician,' he mentioned politely to Hannah. 'He's a Registrar at . . . '

Hannah didn't catch the name of the hospital in question, for Mango had interrupted to ask why Seb had opted for surgery rather than medicine. He shrugged his broad, lightly tanned shoulders and showed his perfect teeth in a grin. 'What a question, coming from you who should know me well enough by now!'

'That's right,' agreed Dickie, 'wouldn't you say we two share the flamboyant temperament of the surgeon? We're the showmen, dicing with death. Jonathan, on the other hand, is a doctor of great intellect, the deep thinker — the brilliant diagnostician. So rumour has it in medical circles. C'mon, let's test Nurse Fitzpatrick and find out if she's really a witch. If she doesn't drown there's our proof.'

They dragged Mango into the pool by her ankles, ignoring her shrieks and Hannah's vain protests, then when they'd finished enjoying themselves clambered out and sat dripping in the sunshine, smoking French cigarettes.

Hannah sat a little apart, out of range of their puffs of smoke, absorbed in her own thoughts, her hands clasped about one bent knee and a slim foot dangling in the sparkling ripples created by the lone swimmer's wake.

Jon pulled himself over the edge, waved aside Dickie's proffered Gitanes and stalked deliberately to Hannah, lowering his towering self until he was beside her on the sun-baked grass, positioned with his back to the others and his attention focused solely on her quiet profile.

A throb of alarm ran through her . . .

'I never cease to be amazed,' he was remarking with a friendly intimacy considering they'd previously exchanged a mere half-dozen words of coolly formal greeting, 'that anyone in the medical world so recklessly continues to smoke. Tell me about yourself.'

Hannah's tongue clove to the roof of her mouth. She could think of not a blind thing to say to this formidable person: and for a girl not generally at a loss for words it was *infuriating* to be so stupidly tongue-tied. Worse still, her body was reacting quite uncontrollably as Jon sprawled casually back, leaning on his elbows, and began to coax the speech to flow once more. He had a voice so low and calm and encouraging that the inner tension relaxed its stranglehold and Hannah began to feel her inhibitions slide away under the spell of such an attentive listener.

Within five minutes there was not much Jonathan Boyd-Harrington did not know about the whole Westcott family; and Hannah had done a complete volte-face where her assessment of the awesome doctor was concerned. Goodhumoured! she found herself marvelling;

and for some odd reason he seemed genuinely interested in her . . .

In breathless fascination she watched as the droplets of moisture evaporated on Jon's warm bronzed skin.

Such unhappiness in his childhood . . . Hannah's hazel eyes were tender with pity. They travelled beyond Jon's Mr Universe shoulders to where Dickie and the others sat chatting and laughing, and occasionally glancing across in their direction. Unconsciously she arched her long neck and stretched her golden limbs in imitation of Mango's practised, seductive poses, tremblingly aware of the way he watched her mouth and her eyes as she spoke.

His own eyes were an unusual purpley-grey, the colour of a gathering stormy sky.

Mango called to Hannah to help her prepare a tray of drinks.

'Thought it was time I broke up that little tête-à-tête,' she teased, intrigued by what she perceived in her friend's dreamy expression.

In the low-ceilinged kitchen with its massive stone walls and cavernous fireplace, the air struck chill on Hannah's bare skin. With an effort she subdued a prickle of irritation at being dragged away from Jonathan.

'He's rather nice,' she murmured casually, and was mortified to hear her friend's knowing laughter. Her full pink mouth settled into a pout as she took the ice cube trays out of the refrigerator, splashed them with hot running water and sloshed ice cubes into the tall jugs of Pimm's Mango was preparing.

'You carry on batting those eyelashes of yours and we'll have him changing his mind about not staying the night . . . Hell's bells, if the girl isn't blushing!'

Hannah tilted a defiant chin. 'Westcotts,' she declared defensively, 'do not blush.' She grimaced at the beat of tell-tale colour in her cheeks. Well, this one hadn't before today. 'My two sisters and I have been brought up to be independent-minded, unshockable, and well able to stand on our own two feet. So there!' Both girls giggled at this pompous little declaration.

'I know, love. But that big beast out there has wolfish instincts and he's clearly thinking you'd make a tender morsel for his supper. Soooo — let's feed and water these brutes and send them on their way. Oops, hold on a moment.' Mango had caught sight of herself in the mirror and was rearranging her chest to better advantage in the black Fiorucci bandeau. 'My lipstick could do with freshening. You go ahead and take the drinks out and I'll be with you in two ticks.'

Smiling happily, Hannah gathered up the laden tray. What a nice day this was turning out to be. Such fascinating visitors. One should never judge by outward appearances: see how wrong she'd been about Jonathan lacking personal warmth.

Humming a gay little tune, she crossed the salon and stepped barefoot out on to the terrace, her steps noiseless as with care she balanced her load of tall glasses, the jugs slopping with ice and chunks of fresh fruit. Rounding the side of the house, she made for the flight of shallow stone steps which turned at right angles to lead on down to the lower gardens and the pool. At their head she paused to steady her precious burden of crystal, just long enough to hear the men's voices echoing up at her from below.

'*Mango!*' that deep mellow voice was scoffing, 'ridiculous name for such a gorgeous girl. Ripe for the plucking, though.'

The answering guffaw of appreciative laughter stopped Hannah dead in her tracks and ideally positioned to overhear every disgraceful word.

Now Dickie was asking, 'What do you think of my Hannah, then? Sweetheart, isn't she? Terrific sense of humour, and brother, can she dance up a storm!'

Hannah's eyes grew wide and her lips parted on a catch of breath.

Seb was most amused. 'Since when have you been interested in *sweet* young girls, Dr Derby? Mango surely is more your style.'

Hannah cringed and bit her lip, squirming against the gritty stone balustrade till it grazed her side, not wanting to hear another word yet unable to make her escape. Her hands were shaking so, it was a wonder no one heard the chink and rattle of the glasses. Her cheeks glowed fiery as red-hot peppers.

Still the girls were the topic under discussion.

'Smashing figure, your Hannah,' conceded Sebastian, 'but next to the other one . . . innocent as a babe in arms. Not at all your type, Dickie, I hope you aren't taking advantage.' More guffaws rent the sultry air.

Please God! prayed Hannah, turn me into a pillar of salt. Strike them dumb. Anything, but please please put a stop to this!

There it was again, that deep, lazy voice vibrating with amusement. 'Did someone say her father's a parson? She looks as if she's been let out of a convent boarding school on a weekend exeat.'

Now Dickie was waxing poetic. 'Darling Hannah comes from a long line of English clerics, brewing their families in rambling country parsonages.'

Hearing this, the convent innocent swore with bitter fluency. 'Derby, you lying creep, how could you!'

'Refined as caster sugar,' observed Jonathan heavily. 'A perfectly composed and well-mannered young English girl. Totally unsuitable for you, Derby. What you should do is hand her over to . . . ' and his quiet voice sank to a lazy basso profundo drawl that Hannah, strain as she might, could not make out.

Oh, but she'd latched on to two horrifying words: *totally unsuitable*! And didn't she just know why he'd said that. Because Hannah Westcott wasn't their sort. Their world was not hers. Marriage to a girl of Hannah's background would not provide the wherewithal to buy Dr Derby into a classy private practice!

Still Hannah dared not move, pinned to the balustrade as surely as a butterfly on a lepidopterist's pin.

'If you're really ambitious, she's the last thing you want hanging round your neck. You've got to keep your options open. Go where the openings occur.'

Hannah's face was a study in anguish. How ruthless! She'd just been dissected — like a specimen on a path lab bench — with all the icy clinical detachment she'd suspected Dr Jonathan Boyd-Harrington was really capable of. Her relationship with Dickie severed — because his career was more important than their love for each other.

And the last straw was Dickie's hasty denial, 'Good grief, man, marriage was the last thing on my mind!'

'Then stay free of ties,' advised Jonathan coolly. 'That's my own philosophy.'

'And Camilla?' interposed Sebastian slyly.

The reproof was pure grated ice. 'You know better than to ask me that.'

Hannah staggered back into the house. Mango was sashaying across the hall in ridiculously high-heeled mules and a cloud of Bal à Versailles. She found the drinks tray thrust unceremoniously into her hands.

'What on earth have you been up to?' she questioned vexedly, then observing the feverish, glittering eyes, 'Are you okay, Han?'

'T-t-too much sun. Going to lie down.'

She took the stairs three at a time: another second and the scalding tears would burst their straining dam.

★   ★   ★

Two days later, when Dickie had gone, Hannah confessed all. Verbatim. With the unanaesthetised pain of total recall.

Mango was gratifyingly outraged. Once the brothers had raced away in their silver monster, heading north for the ferries, Dr Derby had seemed unaccountably restless.

And Hannah had changed into a different person! Snappy, moody, avoiding Dickie and mooning about in her bedroom for hours on end.

'I've no *idea* what's the matter with her! But, my sainted aunt, if this is the real Hannah then . . . ' Words seemed to fail him.

Privately Dickie was patting himself on the back for having listened to Jonathan: it had taken the astute eye of an older man to spot Hannah's essential naïvety. And now that his eyes had been opened, Dickie was anxious to be off. It was too darned uncomfortable to have those misty eyes following him about so reproachfully. What on earth was wrong with the silly girl? Was it something he was supposed to have done?

'How could I have been so mistaken? I thought he loved me!' wept Hannah in a confusion of tears that might have been over Dickie or Jonathan, or both.

'The whole scene keeps playing itself over and over in my mind like some video nasty that won't switch itself off. Totally unsuitable. Those words are carved in blood on my heart. *Totally unsuitable!* that's what that beastly doctor said.'

'I did warn you Jonathan's no saint,' Mango reminded her. 'As for old Dickie — well, it's high time he got the elbow. He never was good enough for you. Playboy of the medical world, that one. He tried me out first, you know, but I made it quite clear I wasn't interested.'

'Then why did you invite him out here?' snivelled Hannah into a sodden tissue, 'if you dislike him so much.'

Mango pressed a lace-edged square of damask into her friend's blindly groping fingers. 'I hoped you'd go off the fellow if you had him around twenty-four hours a day. And I reckon my plan's worked!'

'Oh!' wailed Hannah, 'do-on't . . . I love him so much.' Nineteen. So young to have to cope with a broken heart. How would she survive in London?

Fiercely she grabbed Dickie's photograph and clutched it to her heaving nightshirt. 'I shall buy the most beautiful frame I can afford,' she hiccuped, her sodden eyelashes sticking together beneath the weight of dissolving mascara and bleeding heart, 'and put dear Dickie in it!'

'Great!' applauded Mango with narrow-eyed relish. 'And then we'll bury him with full rites. You'll see, once we get settled in at the Royal Hanoverian you won't give that wretch another thought. As for Dr Beast, I reckon he's done you a favour.'

Dr Beast. Hannah's swollen lips tightened with grim pleasure. The name was more than apt. 'If I ever clap eyes on *him* again . . . ' Indignation stemmed the flow of her tears.

'That you won't,' promised her friend. 'Now wash your face in cold water and come on down to dinner. We're going to drown our sorrows in pink champagne and compose a character assassination of Super-Doc Jonathan.'

And linking arms, the two of them descended to the salon, and for the next couple of hours gave Jonathan Boyd-Harrington not the benefit of a single kindly thought.

2

Thus Dr Beast ruined Hannah Westcott's romance with Dickie Derby.

But a nurse's life moves at a fast and energy-consuming pace, and by the time Hannah had started her second year of training she acknowledged herself wiser and happier than she would ever have believed possible — after that heartbreaking summer of a year past.

Hannah wore her uniform with pride. What a privilege, she often reminded herself, to be a tiny cog in the historic machinery of the Royal Hanoverian; and to think Helen had walked those wards before her in identical striped cotton and crisp starched apron! Not that the tutors in the nursing school were likely to allow her to forget that Helen had *also* succeeded in picking up the coveted Gold Medal.

And Hannah herself wasn't doing so

badly. Ward reports praised her warm, caring personality and recorded with approval the practical good humour with which she approached the most difficult or unattractive of tasks.

Moreover, wrote the Sister-in-Charge, everyone likes Westcott, staff and patients: a valuable member of the nursing team.

To her credit, Hannah had tried to think charitably of Dr Beast, for he proved troublingly hard to forget. And Dickie's photograph had a permanent place among the family portrait gallery set out on a shelf in Room 38.

But though she swallowed her pride and sent him a couple of cheerful letters, Hannah had heard and seen nothing of Dr Derby since the August morning in Provence when he wished her a breezy goodbye and promised to 'be in touch' as soon as she got back to England.

She'd kind of given up hoping when a year passed by on the calendar, and her twentieth birthday came and went without so much as a card from Oxford.

Because her name came last in the alphabet, Hannah was allocated her summer fortnight of 'leave' in mid-October.

'Your parents' place in France gave me a taste for the sun!' she joked with Mango.

So she saved up every penny to visit an out-of-season Spanish isle, tiny and difficult to reach. Travelling alone and on the cheap. Just enough spare cash to hire a bicycle and explore sandy tracks beckoning the way to deserted beaches where the sea lapped clear and pure as crystal. Where Hannah could spread her towel and with a paperback and a bag of oranges blot out memories of that other holiday fraught with mishap.

The cheap return flight dumped her back in England in the middle of a damp and smoky October night. And by the time Hannah struggled up the stairs of the sleeping Nurses' Home, dawn was edging the City skyline.

A parcel of clean uniforms lay by the door of Room 38. Hannah dug deep in the pocket of her white cotton jacket to find her keys, unlocked the door and with a sandalled toe shoved the string-tied bundle across the threshold. With a deft elbow she flicked the light switch, and her bleary eye was assailed by a lot of red scrawl on the wipe-clean message board fixed to the corridor side of her green-painted door.

Mango, of course, knew Hannah was due back that night. 'Welcome home, St/N. Westcott. Say goodbye to Formentera. Miss Johnson expects you at the 8.30 lecture, but never fear, our cold sponge treatment will see you make it.'

'Would you credit it . . . '

Hannah checked the time. Twenty to three! She shivered and felt the goosepimples break out on bare tanned legs. The shiver turned into a yawn. 'I feel like a swallow who's migrated in the wrong direction!' she grumbled to herself, dragging in her luggage and dumping it on the scarlet Indian dhurri which livened up the study-bedroom and reflected its present occupant's preference for colourful surroundings. Her rainbow-striped duvet looked more plumply inviting than ever. But was it worth even bothering with bed . . . ?

From a shelf above the chest of drawers the family snapshots smiled. 'I must let Mum and Dad know I'm safely back,' said Hannah aloud. She frowned at an obvious gap in her carefully arranged portrait gallery. 'Now I'll just unpack the necessities.'

She opened her suitcase and there, wrapped in a sandy towel, smirked Dickie's handsome gilt-framed features. Hannah wiped his glass image on her sleeve and set him in his place, her pretty face unusually solemn as she recollected her decision. Yes, Dickie's picture must go. She'd mulled over a good deal on this holiday; it had been a time for deep reflection. But . . . not quite yet. Let him stay a while longer.

Jenni's wide smile caught her tired eye and Hannah just had to smile back at her younger sister hugging the wriggling furry body of Delilah. There was Dad in his black cassock with an arm round Mum, pictured at a church fête in the vicarage gardens. A fuzzy snap of Paul, who was once engaged to Helen, but the less remembered about *that* ... thought Hannah with a wry expression. Helen might not like it, but Paul's was a photo Hannah would *never* part with.

And Helen herself on her wedding day, hanging on the arm of her brand-new surgeon husband and looking as blonde and beautiful as a film star.

'Hey ho, back to the grindstone,' said Hannah, opening up the cupboard doors to reveal her little washbasin with the illuminated mirror above. On her tidy desk with its files and textbooks a ready made-up cap was waiting, nestling on her blotter like a little white bird.

'What *do* you look like!' she asked the nut-brown stranger's face reflected back at her. 'And just look at your hair!

Right down on to your shoulders now. Johnnie will have something to say about *that*: Off your collar, Nurse, or it's the yard-arm for you!' Hannah stopped smiling and her mouth relaxed to its slightly pouting contours. Julie Christie mouth, Dickie used to say . . .

★   ★   ★

'Some friend you turned out to be!' grumbled Hannah. 'You might have woken me. I've *never* fallen asleep in a lecture before.'

Over coffee in the cafeteria the two girls were deep in a post-mortem of the solitary delights of Hannah's recent vacation. 'All that washing,' she sighed — then brightened. What better excuse to visit Helen — just a tube ride away in Hampstead — and sample her space-age utility room. It wouldn't be full of damp nappies for a few months yet.

'You'll need to rinse out a bikini for the demo on Wednesday morning,' pointed out Mango with a callous grin. 'Sister Tutor said Dr Harlow will need as much flesh to work on as may decently be displayed. *No need to be coy, nurses: you are, after all, professionals,*' she mimicked.

'I'm not coy! I just don't fancy being pawed by Halitosis Harlow in front of the whole set.' The coffee had a bitter taste. Hannah pushed her cup aside, her mind's eye picturing a scene to make any girl shudder. Her goose-pimpled self shivering on a lecture theatre dais; unenvious faces peering down from tiered ranks of seating as Dr Harlow made use of her scantily clad body for his revision demo of the circulatory system.

'Who volunteered me?' she questioned grimly. 'I know it couldn't have been you, dear pal, since you were sitting right beside me listening to my snores. No, don't tell me, I can guess. Marta Macbride! What I ever did to make an enemy of her I never shall fathom.'

'Miss Johnson was *so* grateful. You know how difficult it is getting us nurses to volunteer for the physiology demos.'

'Huh!' snorted Hannah. It was hard though to feel charitable about Macbride. She wore a sneer whenever she so much as glanced Hannah's way and never wasted an opportunity to make plain her dislike.

Hannah sighed aloud.

It didn't need telepathy to guess why. 'Jealous!' Mango was not one to mince her words. 'Take a look at yourself, then at her. You're very popular and exceedingly bright. And your face wouldn't frighten the horses either. Oh, Macbride is green-eyed all right. Marta the Mamba, I call her. Deadlier than the male.'

A sudden brainwave lit a spark of hilarity in Mango's black eyes. They gleamed with wicked humour. 'Let's not make it *too* much of a treat for Marta the Mamba and Halitosis Harlow. I've had this brilliant idea. Now, just you listen to me . . .'

* * *

One of the young housemen had a singular crush on Nurse Westcott. Discovering they had a mutual passion for theatre-going, Dr Pete Fuller laid siege to Hannah's heart via tickets for the National whenever their off-duty coincided. Such outings usually ended up in the kitchen of the Nurses' Home with Pete hoping for rather more than one goodnight kiss, but having to be thankful for a proficiently mixed cup of Horlicks and a generous plate of meat paste sandwiches.

Pete found Nurse Westcott very stimulating company, but mighty hard to seduce. He was also generally starving. And during Hannah's absence, having some trouble with his new boss, the inconsiderate and demanding Senior Registrar who had recently joined Sir Freddy's medical firm. Hadn't been at the Hanoverian five minutes before he started chucking his weight around. Organisation Man, Pete had christened this paragon of medicine.

'Really, Pete!' protested Hannah, horrified as the sandwiches disappeared down the throat of a ravening wolf. 'You'll give yourself indigestion!'

He was thin as a lath. A long streak of lightning, with a long lean jaw to match and fair hair that flopped untidily into his nice blue eyes. Hannah sometimes felt reminded of a playful unco-ordinated puppy. But she enjoyed Pete's company and his lively, extrovert personality.

Pete's room was within sniffing distance of the kitchens.

'This is no lie,' he insisted, 'they started frying kippers at four this morning. Is it any wonder the damn things are inedible by breakfast time? I've never eaten so badly in all my life.'

In the next breath he'd turned romantic.

'Hannie, my angel, life has been incredibly dull with you away. You'll never know how much I've missed you.'

The object of his affection folded her arms and regarded him with a quizzical half-smile. 'You had *time* to miss me? With this Senior Registrar snapping at your heels? Wasn't that excitement enough for a poor weary houseman?'

Pete chose to ignore this gently mocking rebuke. He'd been saving a special titbit all evening. 'What's all the gossip I've been hearing about you and Barry Harlow? It's the talk of the Residency.' A pair of knowing blue eyes leered up at Hannah. 'Tell me, did you volunteer or did Johnnie dig out the thumbscrews?'

Hannah had enjoyed the show — the musical *Guys and Dolls* — so much she'd been transported to another world. A world where physiology demos had never been heard of. For a moment she looked genuinely puzzled before the implication of Pete's teasing questions dawned . . .

Her face was a comic picture of dismay. All round the Residency, the doctors' live-in quarters — oh no! She clapped her hand to her open mouth.

This evident confusion spurred Pete on to the height of witticism. 'Yes indeed,' he gloated. 'All round the

Residency. There'll be medics queueing up for a refresher course — yes, standing room only in Lecture Room 3 on Wednesday morning. Now, old Harlow's a haematologist. Circulation of the blood . . . mmm, we're all a bit hazy about that. Could do with some revision.'

Hannah clasped her burning cheeks in horror. Was this another of Pete's leg-pulls? Of course it was. But she wouldn't put it past him to put his pals up to something of the kind.

'Just the housemen, sweetheart,' comforted her tormentor through a mouthful of crumbs. 'Our lofty Registrars wouldn't give you a second glance. Beneath their dignity — specially one I could name.'

'Thanks for ruining a smashing evening, Dr Fuller. And now may I draw your attention to the time? You'd best be off. On the stroke of midnight my fairy godmother may turn you into a rat!'

But Pete was in no special hurry. He

glanced at his watch. 'Might as well hang on another five minutes. At the stroke of midnight Cinderella's clothes might drop off — why should Barry Harlow have all the fun?'

He fancied himself as something of an Olivier. The pair of them were little short of stage-struck. But Hannah would not play Juliet to Pete's Romeo; and when he made a grab for her, slender and golden-skinned in her white lawn frock, edging past to clear the table and make a start on the washing up, she brushed aside his questing arms — though not unkindly. For Hannah would never willingly hurt another's feelings. After all, didn't she know only too well what it was to be rejected?

It had occurred to her in quiet moments of reflection that perhaps she would never fall in love again. That the emotional damage might have penetrated just too deep for healing.

If Pete really was going to stay put a while longer, then a change of subject would be more than welcome. 'What's he like, then?' questioned Hannah with apparent eagerness, 'this new man, Sir Freddy's new appointment.' Her eyes signalled burning interest. Anything to take Pete's mind off the regular topic of sex . . .

Pete himself was not long out of medical school. This was the first of the two house jobs required of all newly qualified doctors in their post-Registration year — six months as the humblest member of Sir Freddy Blair's medical firm. When his year of hospital experience was completed, he intended to apply for the trainee general practitioner courses — if he could successfully elbow his way through the crush of applicants.

Now, a formidable new figure had stepped in to dominate the scene. One who was clearly not impressed by the engaging personality of Dr Fuller (who was going to require excellent references to further his career).

'What's he *like* . . . ' Pete echoed with a dramatic rolling of the eyeballs, playing for every ounce of Hannah's sympathy. He leaned across the table and clasped her hand as she sat looking at him with those darkly fringed, melting hazel eyes.

'You know how it is — rushed off my feet all day and half the night. Can you blame me if sometimes I get . . . well, behind myself?'

Yes, Hannah knew how it was. A houseman was the general dogsbody, working all the hours God gave. And as if that wasn't hard enough, Pete must now contend with an unsympathetic Registrar who'd forgotten what it was like when he too had been bottom of the pecking order.

That old Joan of Arc in Hannah surfaced, and she tut-tutted and squeezed Pete's hands and declared that if given half the chance she'd tell his new boss a thing or two.

'What's the name of this bully — this Dr Superior? I'll be on the lookout for him. What did you say his name was?'

'Harrington. Eton and Cambridge

and Bart's, no less, wouldn't you know!'

'Of *course*.' Reluctantly, Hannah was a mite impressed. Must be a bright spark, whoever he was. One of those paragons of excellence who torment junior staff, hound the nurses, and reduce patients to tongue-tied servility.

He'd be short and fat and pompous — with a bald spot showing through his thinning fair hair. And a scrubbed pink complexion.

'What does he look like, Pete?'

'Picture,' described Pete, 'an aristocratic prizefighter with Mr Universe shoulders and eyes like a hawk. He's got a bumpy nose and he sort of examines you with lowered scornful eyelids. Never smiles — except in derision. And sports a hundred and one varieties of silk bow tie. *Hand*-tied, naturally. Oh — mustn't forget the bags under his eyes. God knows what puts *them* there.

'And there you have him — Sir Freddy's blue-eyed boy. Dr Harrington.

Member of the Royal College of Physicians.'

Hannah exclaimed softly, mindful that upstairs other nurses lay sleeping. 'Sounds bad news, Pete old dear. You'll just have to ride this storm out. But tell me . . . how on earth do you manage to get his back up? I mean, what goes wrong?'

'I moon around dreaming of you, of course . . . Ouch, Han, what bony fingers you've got!' Pete tossed the lanky hair back from his forehead, and grimaced with rueful candour. 'We-eell. I did put two patients next to one another who rubbed each other's backs up so much one had a minor stroke.'

'You're not a mind-reader!' protested Hannah indignantly. 'Why should you get the blame for a clash of personalities?'

'Ah, but don't you see — my case histories were inadequate. Big Boy pointed out with some asperity that the incompatibility should have been obvious from the start. Put a rabid leftie in the next bed to a Tory councillor from the shires, and you're asking for fireworks.'

'And what else have you done to displease this paragon of a Registrar?'

An angelic grin accompanied a shrug of skinny shoulders under the brick-red Shetland sweater. 'Sins of omission mainly.' Pete struck his chest with a closed fist. '*Mea culpa, mea culpa.* Some files went missing — mind you, I found them easily enough, left on a locker on Grenville Ward. Forgot some of the tests Sir Freddy ordered on a woman doctor we had in with acute anaemia. Well, he wants everything done yesterday, does Jon.'

'You ought to make lists,' said Hannah severely. 'Who's John?'

'Jon Harrington. I told you. I've been late for ward rounds, lost path lab samples and the odd X-ray. Oh, he isn't impressed with me, our Organisation Man. What he fails to take into account is that I probably haven't been to bed for three days when these — er

— mishaps occur. You want to try being a model of efficiency on my schedule!'

A warm hand squeezed Pete's comfortingly. 'He was a houseman once upon a time. And he must have noticed what a way you have with the patients. It cuts far more ice with a sick person to be treated with kindness and good humour than a battery of nasty tests. You're going to be a smashing family doctor, so don't let Organisation Man sap your confidence. You're exhausted, Pete, *not* inept.'

Hannah produced her keys with an air of finality and shepherded Pete to the main door. 'In four months this chap will just be a nasty memory. I'll see you keep your chin up. Never fear, Doctor dear.'

Alone in the kitchen, finishing the stack of unwashed crocks left in the sink by thoughtless nurses entertaining boyfriends, Hannah pondered over Pete's problems. Trouble was, if you didn't know him very well, that tendency to act the goon could make an unfortunate first impression. Dr Harrington might not yet have come to realise that the jocular side of Dr Fuller's personality did not impair the seriousness of his professional concern for their patients.

All the same, mused Hannah with a shake of her thoughtful head, rinsing all the mugs left for Billy Muggins to clear away and stacking them in a cupboard, it was most unkind of this Harrington chap to take on the rôle of hard task-master sorting out the hospital buffoon. Pete was greatly liked . . . and heavens above, how did you survive in the hospital world without a sense of humour?

The Senior Registrar had managed to climb the ladder in spite of lacking the ability to smile. Hannah thought she'd formed a very clear impression of this mirthless man; I don't suppose *your* company is much sought after, Doctor! she informed the faceless new member of the medical staff. I shouldn't imagine you'll fit in here at the Royal Hanoverian . . . bulldozing your animal frame along our corridors. No, I don't relish the prospect of clapping eyes on *you*.

'Poor old Pete,' she murmured aloud, then switched off all the lights and went up to her dark little room.

★   ★   ★

'If you're going to look an idiot, might as well make the most of it!' had been Mango's advice. 'Give us all a giggle, eh, Han? Better than boring the pants off the whole set. Johnnie won't mind — there's a sense of humour under all the starch.'

Suddenly Hannah wasn't so sure of that, waiting now in the lecture theatre, wrapped in her big cloak and standing barefoot on the far side of the rostrum looking out through the wall of windows to the netless tennis courts with their carpet of sodden brown and gold leaves.

In spite of the central heating and the heavy wool of her cloak, she was shivering slightly, awaiting the arrival of the tardy Dr Harlow.

Miss Johnson had finished her own

preparations and was pursing her strict mouth at the prospect of an unprompt start.

Hannah found to her surprise that far from being apprehensive she was actually rather bored. Wasting time irritated her; she preferred to be working. So she stared out of the window and slipped into an imaginary dream world, relaxing, wriggling her toes against the polished wooden boards and pretending sunbaked sand was sifting over her bare feet.

Once she looked upward and saw Mango beaming down conspiratorially. Mango had found the bikini. Sensational really. If you happened to be an oversized wasp!

So it was that when the door flew open and an instant hush fell upon the throng of chattering nurses, a dreamy-eyed Hannah didn't notice a thing. Gazing out of the window at leaden skies, and wondering at the speed with which Christmas was approaching . . . the second Christmas away from her family in their gaunt

64

Victorian city vicarage.

An intrigued silence held the whole place in thrall. The doctor finished conferring with Miss Johnson and strode to the centre of the rostrum, relaxed and confident, his lopsided grin enveloping each and every nurse present.

'I'm very glad to have this opportunity to meet you all today.'

The voice, deep and resonant, reached into every corner and thrilled every heart.

Every heart that was, except one. Even Miss Johnson looked smitten.

But one girl had heard that special timbre roll through her dreams too often to forget. Her throat shrivelled dry as a desert. Each drop of blood sprang to attention. And slowly Hannah turned to face the stranger on the rostrum.

Not Dr Harlow.

'Especially since some of you have assignments on the medical wards following this study block.'

Fifty-eight nurses exchanged coos of interest. Who was this strikingly attractive new doctor?

Nurse Fitzpatrick was chewing her fingernails — for she knew the answer to the thousand-dollar question and her concern was all for Hannah. From the moment he strode authoritatively into the lecture theatre and launched himself on to the dais with a lithe athletic spring, Mango had been staring down from the ranks in horrified disbelief. It *couldn't* be! Surely fate couldn't be that cruel . . .

And down there waited Hannah, all unsuspecting, daydreaming of God knows what, her cloak wrapped tight about her and that monstrous get-up about to be revealed for the supposed delectation of a sweating Dr Harlow.

Jonathan Boyd-Harrington, Member of the Royal College of Physicians, set his long legs comfortably astride and thrust his hands into his trouser pockets. He rarely lectured with notes. He didn't need to.

The open jacket displayed an impressively broad expanse of cream silk Turnbull and Asser, closed at the throat by a scarlet bow-tie. The contrast with the way Mango remembered him, in Bermuda shorts and slither of swim trunks, was almost shocking in its transformation.

'Wow!' exclaimed Nurse Fitzpatrick on an indrawn breath.

More sophisticated than her fellow nurses, she recognised the cut of Savile Row tailoring, the way finest navy worsted with discreet chalk-stripe smoothed the outline of developed muscles and skimmed over the strength of rock-hard thighs. The physique of a navvy, recalled Mango, who had been privileged to observe that body stripped off under a pulsating French sun . . .

And it belonged to the one man whom Hannah Westcott, in spite of her loving nature, had allowed herself to loathe.

'First,' the doctor was continuing now, innocently straightfaced, 'I must apologise for depriving you all of Dr Harlow's expertise.'

For once Miss Johnson's formidable frown was insufficient to quell the ripple of approval swelling from fifty-eight throats.

She stepped swiftly to Dr Harrington's side.

'Ladies! Dr Harlow has been called to an emergency and I am delighted to introduce the new Senior Registrar on Sir Frederick's firm — Dr Jonathan Boyd-Harrington, who wishes to be known simply as Dr Harrington. It is particularly appropriate since, as Dr Harrington has reminded us, you are about to commence your second period of duty on the medical wards. So very kind of you, Doctor, to step in at such short notice and fill the breach. And here is your model, Nurse Hannah Westcott.'

'Good morning . . . Hannah.'

Beneath the cloak Hannah was trembling like an aspen sapling in a north wind.

John Harrington, then, was none other than Jonathan Boyd-Harrington. She simply hadn't made the connection, had no earthly reason to suppose their paths might ever cross again.

Yet here he stood, not two feet away, towering over her and Johnnie, elegantly raffish, and oh, so sure of himself. So close Hannah could smell the tang of lemony soap and a trace of Givenchy Gentleman.

. . . A gentle man? Not on your life!

Numb with shell-shock, Hannah squinted helplessly up at Dr Beast's affably brutal profile . . .

Vanished on the instant, all memory of the conviction reached on the sunny beaches of Formentera where she'd patted herself on the back for being mature and magnanimous in vowing to put the past behind her — told herself that even if he *had* asked her, no sensible girl would have risked marrying the like of Dr Derby. The lesson had been learned most painfully. But Mango was right and the wicked Dr Harrington had in truth done Hannah a favour . . .

On the platform of Lecture Room 3 all those good resolutions turned to so much candy floss. This man towering over her was a villain. He was terrorising Pete, her kind and well-meaning *friend*!

Joan of Arc armed herself for battle.

It quite escaped Hannah's train of thought that houseman and Registrar are to each other as teacher and pupil. Theoretically the consultants are contracted to teach junior medical staff as they continue their training in house jobs; in practice it is the Registrars who fit such teaching into their own hectic working schedules. And Jon Harrington was undertaking to pass on his own knowledge and experience to Hannah's friend Pete. Pete — inclined to be scatty and a practical joker, and undoubtedly requiring a firm hand to keep him organised and on the ball.

'Cloak off, Nurse,' said Miss Johnson briskly, while Hannah like a drowning man saw her past life surge through her inner vision. Bravely she lifted defiant eyes to the dread stranger who had so callously scuttled her first yearning love affair and then walked out of her life without so much as a backward glance.

She glanced scornfully across at Macbride, slouching in the front row alongside her cronies and as bowled over by the lecturer as everyone else in the room. Everyone who knew no better!

Hannah's burning gaze travelled back to Dr Harrington. Typical! The way that whole image proclaimed power. Look at me, I am accustomed to being obeyed. Look, but keep your mouths shut and just do as I say. I am not to be argued with. You are all my handmaidens. Jump when I say jump.

The Beast! she agonised as her heart pounded against the prison of her ribs. He's quite aware it's the usual female reaction. See how his mouth quirks as he looks up at all those stupidly sighing nurses. Wait till the Hanoverian gets to know you better, Jon Harrington!

Lazy purple-grey eyes suddenly turned upon Hannah the victim, regarding her from beneath heavy, speculative lids.

The broad brow scarred with thought.

A strong hand stroked the assertive jawline as Harrington dredged his sub-conscious for a near-forgotten memory . . .

His first conscious sight of the nurse had been an odd one: there was this gaping mouth in a shocked brown face, shrugged up to the ears in the enveloping folds of a navy cloak — just a glimmer visible of ticklish scarlet lining. There was a mass of shiny bronzed hair — which was not how nurses usually presented themselves! — tumbling over the collar. And most intriguing of all, two accusing hazel eyes, sumptuously fringed with lashes of a darker hue than that streaky gold-brown hair would generally warrant, registering Shock. Disbelief. And an almost tangible sense of wishing their owner — or the doctor himself! — a thousand miles away.

Jon's eyebrows drew together. What a curious creature. No one else seemed to mind about Barry Harlow . . .

The Senior Registrar was well accustomed to thinking on his feet, and a master of the swift diagnosis. Had Jon only known how wide of the mark his judgment was on this occasion . . . but his intelligent brow cleared with the characteristic certainty of the highly experienced physician. Confident that he had hit upon what must be piquing his now sullenly pouting model, he regarded Hannah with a quizzical, mildly amused, eye.

So Harlow's your current flame, is he, the lucky devil? Bit of a shock to have me turn up, eh! No doubt the two of you were counting on a bit of extra-curricular fun, and all in the line of duty. Shame! 'Right, Nurse,' Jon murmured aloud, but for Hannah's ears only. 'Off with your clothes and let's get this show on the road.'

'What a hunk!' whispered Marta excitedly, nudging her companions and giggling. 'And doesn't Westcott look *miserable*! This is going to be even better than I'd hoped!'

Hannah stepped into the centre of the platform, that old stubborn streak freezing all emotion other than a cool bravado. No one was going to get the chance to suspect her inner turmoil; except Mango, biting her nails at the drama down on the dais. As for Jon Harrington, Hannah thought she'd picked up a flicker of something in his careful scrutiny. But she was pretty sure he hadn't recognised her as the girl by the pool in France.

Her cloak fell dramatically to the floor . . .

The model was supposed to present plenty of bare skin for the doctors to delineate muscles and organs and blood vessels, and scrawl with their red and blue (washable) pens as they taught student nurses the way around the human body.

. . . Purple-grey eyes narrowed.

Miss Johnson's tongue clicked.

A titter went up from the front row and quickly spread to the back tier. Hannah couldn't stop herself from grinning back, and catching sight of this Mango sank back against her seat with a sigh of relief. Things were certainly not working out as planned, but thank heaven Westcott had a sense of humour and wasn't the sort to crumple into a soppy heap at a setback.

Mango stuck a thumb up in encouragement, and Hannah nodded a glossy, tousled head in reply.

'Well, well,' murmured Jon Harrington in his soft and mellow bass, 'I trust this bathing dress is not a valued *antique*, since I'm about to draw patterns all over you.'

He had his back half-turned to the audience as Sister Tutor moved her chair across to the side of the dais.

'Do just as you please,' returned Hannah icily, adding sotto voce, 'as is your usual wont.'

She was calming down rapidly as the surface of her bare skin chilled to room temperature. Not that *too* immodest an expanse of biscuity flesh was visible in the grossly striped stretch-nylon top and the hideous drawers which clung to her thighs.

All of a sudden it seemed less funny to be standing there looking like a clown. And something about the set of Miss Johnson's mouth suggested trouble. Worst of all, Hannah was struggling with the despicable feeling that if she could only have *known* the formidable Dr Harrington was going to do this demo, she'd have worn something far more attractive!

Firm hands grasped Hannah by the shoulders and propelled her to the front of the rostrum. The demonstration had begun.

She was obliged to submit to being manhandled this way and that as coloured pens provided by Miss Johnson traced major arteries and delineated the contours of muscles. Dr Harrington even threw in, gratis, a history lesson about how back in the seventeenth century William Harvey, physician to the Stuart kings, discovered the systemic circulation of the blood. It was fascinating stuff, and his audience were leaning forward so as not to miss a word, eagerly responding to quick-fire questioning designed to test their recollection of work covered in the first year of training.

Soon Hannah looked even more bizarre than she had intended. Most of what Dr Harrington was saying had frozen into incomprehension as her body fought to deny reality. The hands of the enemy were warm and decisive as they manipulated her arms and legs, shoulders and neck, tracing patterns over her torso, designing grotesque red and blue circles round the wasp-striped bra cups with all the cheerful indifference of a man handling a shop dummy.

'Roll that waistband right down over your hipbones,' ordered Dr Harrington. 'You were surely told to wear something much more brief to let me get at you.'

He lowered his voice to an intimate murmur. 'No tidemarks to this very becoming tan, Nurse Westcott — all-over, is it?'

Hannah could hardly believe her ears! Hot fury dissolved the core of icy detachment that had held her head high. And it took a mighty effort of will not to stalk offstage in outrage and rush straight back to the safety of the Nurses' Home. Her bottom lip quivered for just a moment, then thrust out in characteristic determination not to let Harrington sense her humiliation. She glanced down at the black ice of his immaculate toecaps and held herself tense and untrembling.

'Let's have you on a chair. This is giving me backache.'

'Terminal, I hope!' muttered the defiant Nurse Westcott. She clambered in ungainly fashion on to the seat indicated, her rude retort echoing harmlessly in her own ears — for Dr Harrington was occupied with dictating a paragraph for the class's lecture notes.

Then he attacked her again with a chunky red pen, outlining her liver and standing there with nonchalant finger-tips resting on her left hipbone — just as if she were the demo-skeleton from the School of Nursing — while he rapped out a question that Mango was answering with disgraceful alacrity. My best friend, thought Hannah gloomily, thanks for knifing me in the back, Brutus.

Mango, however, was secretly hugging herself in hilarious admiration. That outfit was a scream! And even more so, since Hannah was posing with all the professional disdain of a Parisian mannequin with that terrific figure of hers, behaving just as if she might be modelling haute couture for one of the more daring fashion houses.

'If you're just acting, Han,' she exulted, 'then, kid, you must be the greatest!' Specially since *inside* Hannah must be absolutely seething.

Unless . . . wondered Mango slowly as an interesting thought began to take shape. Unless it was turning out to be perversely thrilling to have the beastly Jonathan Boyd-Harrington, Eton and Cambridge and Guy's or wherever, designing his model's heart all over again with his sensuous red pens. Less romantic, of course, to see that heart in its true anatomical size and shape and position. And of course to poor Hannah it must be as if bleeding arrows were stabbing her, through and through.

'This young lady is very thin,' announced Dr Harrington blithely, with scant consideration for his captive's ill-concealed wince of chagrin. He swivelled Hannah about — this was especially precarious for someone balancing on a chair with uneven legs — and unfastened her bandeau top. 'Hold this out of the light, there's a good girl.' He proceeded to bend her over and run a ruler along her vertebrae in such a swashbuckling manner that the bony twang made Hannah shudder and set her teeth on edge.

'All the easier,' he continued, 'when I place her sideways — thus — to observe the perfect curve of a strong, healthy back.'

Hannah stood sideways, grinding her jaws with the effort it was taking not to boot Harrington where it would be most effective. For dear life she hung on to her horrible nylon wasp top, praying cravenly for the lecture to end.

That night in the nurses' sitting room everyone else was eager for a post-mortem.

'Bet you were enjoying yourself!'

'Lucky so-and-so.'

'Ben Surfleet says he's not married!'

No one seemed particularly interested in the chess set, or in Clint Eastwood being murderously impassive on the TV screen.

Hannah's skin still smarted from the soapy nailbrush she had scoured herself with under a hot shower.

'Miss Johnson assured me these are washable inks, Hannah,' he had observed, quite kindly, at the end of the session. Using her Christian name with all the aplomb of the lord and master dismissing his soiled handmaiden to her ablutions. Then he had placed the big cloak over her shoulders — with a gallantry entirely out of keeping with his beastly image, in his attentive scrutiny a gleam of something which had Hannah pretending particular concern with the neatness of her sensible shoelaces.

The last thing she wanted to read in those intrusive eyes was that she had indeed been recognised. Of course her name was fairly unusual. But wasn't it more than likely that a 'slip of a kid' (from a vicarage of all places) would have been ejected from Boyd-Harrington's memory *tout-de-suite?*

No, decided Hannah, chewing on her

lower lip. Better all round if I keep my distance and fade into the wallpaper like the obliging little church mouse I'm expected to be. But . . . what if Jon Harrington bumps into Mango? He's never going to have forgotten *her*!

'I'm afraid,' commiserated Mango over a bedtime cocoa in Hannah's room, 'that it'd look a bit odd if our paths cross and I don't say Hi! Our families — *you* understand.'

'Of course,' agreed Hannah quickly, secretly hoping that in a place as huge as the Hanoverian that might never happen. With apparent indifference she smoothed moisturising cream over her long brown legs. All she wanted was to creep beneath the safe warmth of her duvet and blot out this whole impossible day.

Hannah's sudden jawbreaking yawn of sheer weariness made her friend drain her cocoa and scramble to her feet from beside the gas fire. ''Night, then. Happy dreams and sweet repose, and dream of nice things under the clothes — as my granny used to say to me at bedtime.'

May I have a deep and dreamless sleep tonight, prayed Hannah with silent but understandable fervour.

In the corridor outside, Mango hesitated. Was Hannah really okay?

She had been so silent, not at all her usually chatty self. And she hadn't wanted to discuss Jon Harrington full stop. Most disappointing! *And,* speculated Mango with furrowed black brows, how long had Dickie Derby's picture been consigned to the rubbish bin?

The click of the light switch and the sound of slippered feet padding across to the bed reassured Mango and she went thoughtfully to her own room, troubled ever since that holiday in France by a sense of responsibility for all that had befallen Hannah as guest of the Fitzpatricks.

Some twenty minutes later, Hannah sighed, flat on her back and eyes staring into the darkness, still wide awake. Here, alone, with only her teeming thoughts for company, sleep was proving wickedly elusive.

She remembered how at lunch break she'd come storming back to her room and in irritation had seized hold of Dickie's photograph and dropped it with a decisive clatter into the wastepaper bin.

Now she'd had a change of plan. Back went the covers, and her feet padded over the red rug to the waste bin by her desk. Out came Dickie. 'Too good a frame to waste,' said Hannah grimly, prising off the cardboard backing and crumpling the smirking doctor into a ball. She tossed Dickie back into the debris of her life, smacking the palms of her hands like cymbals. Good riddance. Her eyes alighted on the textbook *Practical Procedures for Nurses.* A highly practical procedure — and long overdue. From now on it would be the sensible and rational Student Nurse Westcott — with one interest in life: nursing. And sex? Pity such a time-wasting occupation was ever invented.

Hannah crossed to the window and stared out over the glow of London by night. 'I've learned something today,' she informed herself wryly. 'Dr Beast is more hateful for behaving like an ogre and wiping that tonic of a grin off Pete's face than for what he did to hurt me in France. That must be telling me something!' she yawned hugely. 'Though all of a sudden I'm too tired to work out just what.'

3

'You'll love working on Grenville!' panted Pete, loping by in the opposite direction as he headed for Path Lab with the morning's collection of blood and urine samples for testing. 'Ellen French is a honey, and so's Staff Phillips. Look, I've got to fly, have a nice day!' he called American-fashion, half walking, half running backwards, white coat flying, arms laden. 'Don't forget the audition tomorrow for the Christmas panto — *Beauty and the Beast*. Over in the medical school. You've got to audition for . . . '

'Back row of the chorus!' called back Hannah. She hurried on and the smile slipped from her anxious face. First day on Grenville. Harrington territory. Butterflies in the tummy. The navy petersham belt nipped her narrow waist and the starched collar at her throat constricted. She always felt a heightening of adrenalin, hastening to report for duty on a new ward; today there was this peculiar sensation of dread.

The cheek of it, she recalled indignantly — saying I was very thin!

For goodness' sake, Hannah scolded herself, what a time to be thinking about Dr Beast. No, your belt isn't too tight, you're just a bit nervous and you know that won't last five minutes once you're in Sister French's office.

You are thin, though. You lost almost a stone last year after that break-up with Dickie. Remember when Johnnie called you to her office and demanded to know if you were turning anorexic? And you got such a shock because she'd noticed that you went home and ate double helpings of turkey and plum pud.

I can eat like a pig and it makes no difference! My metabolism burns up the calories as fast as I shovel them down.

Well, fine then — if you don't mind

Jon Harrington thinking you're unattractively thin . . .

I should care! Hannah told herself crossly, squeezing into the crowded lift with her fingers crossed. She hated lifts. But Grenville was on the third floor of the Wymark building.

Do you think he recognised you? Perhaps he noticed you were thinner . . .

He hadn't exactly said, 'Why, if it isn't that nice *refined* little mouse I met one summer in Provence!' No, he'd just left her in a condition of confused resentment, wondering did he or did he not recognise his enemy Hannah Westcott.

In the staff lavatory Hannah pegged her cloak alongside the others, straightened her cap and smoothed her skirts, felt in her pocket for notebook and pen, and went in search of Sister's office. This was her second assignment on a medical ward, so she knew what would be expected of her. She was here to build on the skills learned in the first year and to undertake more demanding techniques of patient care. She had already decided she preferred medical to surgical nursing. The nursing process really came into its own where patients were admitted for longer stays. More time to form relationships with sick people, whose treatment would be lengthier and less dramatic than the surgeon's knife. Hannah enjoyed that. Such a ward would be highly organised and meticulous, without the bustle and planned disruption of surgeons' lists. She liked that, too.

Outside the office Hannah squared her shoulders, knocked and entered. Sister French, flanked by the night staff, was poring over the Kardex, and among the group of day nurses Hannah saw Macbride, long pale face smirking at having beaten Westcott to it. Just my luck, she commiserated with herself, to get the same assignment as Marta.

With a nod to the newcomer, Sister concluded her discussion with warm thanks to the two night nurses for their hard work on her patients' behalf — which was nice of her, thought

Hannah, some Sisters didn't take the trouble — and started on briefing the day staff.

When at length she and Marta stood alone before Ellen French's desk, Hannah could feel the tension in the back of her knees. But she couldn't repress the habitual smile in her eyes or the alert eager expression illuminating her candid features. Macbride, noted Ellen French with foreboding, had the kind of features that fell readily into a frown, and her fingernails were bitten to the quick. She looked plain glum.

'As you already know,' Sister said briskly, 'our work on a medical ward is always varied and interesting.'

Macbride coughed boredly behind her hand. What *she* knew was that the next eight weeks were going to prove a real pain. Medical wards were a hotch-potch of complaints. The operating theatre was where Marta couldn't wait to be. She watched Westcott get out her pocket notebook and rapidly take down the information Sister was dishing out about various patients and their treatment. Marta's thin lip curled.

'We take general medical cases here on Grenville.' Ellen French had nice brown eyes and a healthy complexion, more like a countrywoman than the Londoner she was born and bred. Her fair hair curled neatly and naturally under the froth of lace that designated her a Sister-in-Charge. Hannah's pencil paused and she momentarily lost the thread as she examined Ellen French as closely as politeness allowed. Someone said she had three young children. Imagine that! . . .

' . . . admit patients requiring particularly specialised treatment, though a case may be transferred from here to a surgical ward. We have, for example, a Mr Heron who is not responding to treatment for thyroid. Dr Harrington has decided surgery will be the only answer.'

That dreaded name — so casually introduced!

Hannah's lips tingled as if bloodless.

She dipped her head to conceal the sudden pallor, and the sensation that she'd been struck by lightning. Grenville, of course, was one of his wards, and her stomach had been churning since she first opened her eyes and remembered what day it was. If Harrington caught her reacting like this he might mistake her confusion for some kind of silly girlish crush.

Imagine it. Such an appalling mistake!

Pulses pounding, Hannah made an enormous effort to concentrate on Sister's calm voice. To her relief, the phone on the desk shrilled urgently and the two found themselves dismissed to seek out Staff Nurse Phillips.

'And please read the Grenville handbook from cover to cover. In your own time, nurses,' were Ellen French's parting words.

At ten-thirty they were dismissed to a ten-minute coffee break, seeking refuge in the sluice for a breather since there wasn't time to go off the ward. Hannah gave up attempting to chat to Macbride — an effort about as enjoyable as wading through cold porridge — and buried her nose in the ward handbook.

Crunch! She glanced up in distraction to see Marta sinking her fangs into a polished green Granny Smith apple. Marta caught her stare and pulled a face; much she cared about Sister's ban on her nurses eating the patients' fruit. An old chap, privately thinking to himself that a dose of vitamin C would improve the new nurse's pasty complexion, had pressed upon the girl an apple from the bowl on his locker. Marta hadn't hesitated to accept.

'That's it, me ducks, pop it in yer pocket. I got plenty o' fruit left — and me daughter she'll bring more in tonight. An' take one for your boyfriend down there. I seen you watching him. He's a good 'un, young Dr Pete. Makes yer laff — an' don't a body feel better for it!'

Chuckling wheezily, he nodded towards Pete, who was busy farther along the ward.

'Him?' Marta had grimaced. 'He's already spoken for.' She had nodded in Hannah's direction, bitterly aware that a girl like herself was never likely to earn a second look from Dr Fuller. He was no oil painting, mind, but there was something very attractive about the lean humorous lines of his face and the way his floppy hair fell in his eyes as he leaned over to examine a patient. *Westcott* just had to flutter those dizzy eyelashes of hers to have Pete panting devotedly at her elbow . . .

All the same, meditated Marta with a sly glint in her eye, trailing behind plump, dark-skinned Staff Phillips as she led the way to the utility room, while I'm stuck here on Grenville there's bound to be a chance to liven things up for Hannah and Pete. Marta smiled thinly to herself with malicious satisfaction, knowing she was as adept with the wooden spoon as with the knife between the shoulderblades.

Now she watched with a sneer as Hannah read aloud the crash call procedure for Grenville Ward. 'We'll have to stay on in our own time to get through this lot.'

'Catch me!' The apple core slewed across the sluice in the general direction of the disposal bin, missed and splattered on the polished grey vinyl tiles. Marta wiped her hands on her apron and wandered off to the cloak-room.

Sister French, wrapped in her cloak for the trip across to Admin, looked into the sluice and nodded as she saw the new nurse intently studying the handbook of ward procedure. Her expression stiffened as she saw the apple core and the sticky mess on the floor. 'Patients' fruit, I imagine,' she said grimly, and Hannah's stomach gave a lurch of dismay. She couldn't get Macbride into deliberate trouble.

'I — er — I was just about to clear that up, Sister,' she stuttered lamely.

'Then do it immediately, Nurse. When the lunches come up don't forget to plug the trolley into the electric point out here in the passage. I shall be across in Admin for half an hour. If Dr Harrington appears before I'm back, tell him I particularly want to have a word about Mr Kenton's medication. Don't let him shoot off without seeing me.'

Hannah pressed a hand to her mouth in dismay. Where was Staff Nurse Phillips? How on earth was a student nurse expected to give orders to a senior doctor? What should she do to detain him? Swing from his white coat? Throw herself across the ward doors with her arm thrust through the two bars?

The very doors opened before her eyes, and in walked Pete carrying a rack of test tubes and a red carnation. 'Hannah, my poppet, are you surviving? Look what I've brought you, fresh from the florist.' He thrust the flower down her apron front, and Hannah forgot all her worries as damp soaked through to her bra.

'You pinched that from a vase, you

horror, Pete Fuller! I bet that's stinking water running all down my chest!

Hampered by the test tubes, Pete made an investigatory lunge with his left hand. 'Can't have that, can we, young feller!' he leered in an Archers of Ambridge accent. 'Get ye into the sluice and I'll have a quick check for ye.' He wondered why Hannah was acting so jittery and staring bug-eyed at a point somewhere above his shoulder. Sister was off the ward: he'd passed Frenchie on the way up, so the coast was clear.

Hannah was grappling as if to defend her honour. The swing doors had parted abruptly, and there stood Jon Harrington, his features stiff with shock as he encountered his houseman apparently about to rip the dress off a struggling young Grenville nurse. Oh oh! *That* nurse . . .

'Dr Fuller!'

Pete swung round, cradling the test tubes in defensive arms.

'Is this man bothering you, Nurse?'

'N-no,' gulped Hannah, her hands flying to her buttons and her shoulders heaving with a peculiar breathlessness. 'I — er — it's only Pete . . . my — '

Jon looked the two of them up and down with a slow sardonic eye. 'Quite,' he responded with heavy sarcasm. 'If you would care to join me . . . Pete!' He strolled past in the direction of the office, and the irreverent Dr Fuller pulled a hilarious grimacing face behind that broad implacable back, and dutifully followed.

'OK, chief!' he murmured smartly, just out of earshot and winking reassuringly at Hannah, who was biting her lip and frowning in anxiety.

The two men went into the doctors' room — a small office equipped with easy chairs, a desk, telephone and typewriter. The door shut to with a curt and dismissive snap.

Hannah glanced up and down the corridor before tiptoeing across and placing an ear against the unpainted dark wood; but whatever his temper, Dr

Harrington was not about raising that quiet voice he had so painstakingly trained to speak low and slow. It had come about when he realised in his first youthful contact with patients that because of his size and build, people were genuinely timid in his presence. It had taken determination on Jon's part to succeed; but his wrath was all the more effective for rarely coming over strong, a quietly icy tongue-lashing that left the recipient in no doubt of the wisdom of keeping on the right side of Dr Harrington.

Hannah couldn't see or hear a thing; but she could just picture the scene. Pete in his limp white coat with his hands folded behind his back, saying all the right things — yes, sir, no, sir, very sorry, sir. Jonathan Harrington in his dark grey pinstripe with the snowy double-cuffed shirt and plum silk bow-tie, arms folded, brawny legs akimbo, planted smack in front of the window and scowling disapproval upon his scatty young houseman.

She hadn't got it quite right. Both men were sitting and Jon, with a quick glance at his watch, was suggesting that possibly a meaty part in the Royal Hanoverian's annual pantomime might provide an outlet for the more frivolous side of Dr Fuller's nature.

Pete's mouth twitched. Just occasionally he suspected his boss's tongue might be in his cheek; this was one such moment. The Registrar moved on to tackle the bed situation on Grenville.

'I'm not at all happy about putting a man in terminal liver failure next to a much younger chap with cirrhosis.'

Pete leaned forward eagerly. 'I'd like to justify that if I may. It's my belief that the temperaments of these two men are actually a comfort and support. Old Sam knows well enough that the situation's hopeless. The stomach growth has spread to the liver and he's in here till he dies. But my word, he's a serene and cheery old boy — and his brand of highly unprofessional counselling is doing Mr Beevers more good than a whole coven of medical social workers.'

The Registrar was looking thoughtful. 'What do you consider will be the effect on Beevers when very shortly the old man goes into a hepatic coma? The chief and I agree we should let him see his time out here on Grenville where he's happy and familiar with all the staff.'

'Sir, I think that Mr Beevers' attitude is much more positive now — thanks to our Sam. He's eager to cooperate; has even agreed to psychiatric help. The injections of concentrated vitamins and the high-protein diet have helped build him up, and his wife is now being much more supportive.'

'And when Sam goes into coma he can be wheeled into a side ward . . . '

'Sorry to interrupt,' said Hannah, knocking and entering, 'but might Sister have a word with you before you go, Dr Harrington? She's in her office.' With the message duly delivered and responded to, she turned and fled to the safety of the ward, assured that Pete was in one piece and that Jon Harrington hadn't given her a glimmer of recognition. Apart from recalling her surname, revealed among other things on that fatal Wednesday morning.

'Who is that nurse, Fuller?'

'Friend of mine, sir, Hannah Westcott,' said Pete, gratified to have his Registrar's interest. And no wonder, smirked Pete; Hannah's tanned and freckly face was a picture just then, peeping round the door at them, a vision of health and youthful perfection.

Jon's black brows contracted in a scowl and he looked far from pleased. For a girl who'd made such a strong initial impression that day in France, the sun behind her and wreathed in starry flowers, she was turning out to have the most appallingly injudicious taste in men. Clearly, though, that Derby fellow had been given his marching orders — to be replaced by this amiable, gangling houseman. Most unfortunate to have her here on Grenville, taking the houseman's disorganised mind off his job.

There was a moment or two of heavy silence during which the Registrar considered the desirability of transferring Nurse Westcott to the ward of another medical firm, out of harm's way. He decided, though, to deal with the problem here and now. Doctor/Nurse relationships were regrettable at the best of times; impossible on the same ward. 'Just don't mess around with that girl here on Grenville. If I catch any more monkey business, Fuller, you're for the high jump. Right?'

Pete gulped, aghast at the other's volte-face.

'And if you want my advice — and you're getting it whether you like it or not — never tangle with nurses. Confine your sex life to women outside the hospital gates. And I repeat, avoid Hannah Westcott like the plague when you're working on Grenville. Or I shall have your guts for garters!'

Inside Pete was fuming. But what could he do? A bad report from Harrington and he might as well go jump in the Serpentine. Just wait till he reported back to Hannah — she'd be livid at such blatant interference.

Dr Harrington strode off to Sister's office, his brow furrowed as a medieval field, his mouth a grim line of disapproval. Medicine — the patients — must come first. There was no room for flippancy on the wards of the Royal Hanoverian.

And Hannah, glimpsing Jon's refrigerated features from the safety of the kitchen as she poured a glass of milk for old Sam, shivered at her misfortune in being condemned to Grenville for eight whole weeks, with Jonathan Harrington dominating every watchful working hour.

★   ★   ★

'Hannah! We thought you were coming across for the auditions. What's keeping you?'

Hannah glanced up from her essay on functions of the liver and pancreas, eyes blurred from concentrating on the small print of the textbook. The girl in the doorway was flushed with exertion, a hospital cape flung over her short shorts and tee-shirt, high heels teetering on the threshold of Hannah's room.

It was quite an outfit, and Hannah smiled. 'I must be too late now,' she admitted. 'Oh well, that's that. I forgot the time, Wendy, but I did mean to come. It was such terrific fun last year. Ah well . . . '

Wendy advanced and grabbed Hannah by the arm. 'Leave that for now,' she urged. 'We haven't got a pianist and we want to run through one of the dance routines. Afraid I volunteered you. Please come — it's hopeless without music.'

Resignedly Hannah shut her books and allowed herself to be hustled through the damp dark night and across to the medical school where the examinations hall had been commandeered for rehearsals. Dog-eared sheet music was thrust before her at the keyboard and she plunged into sight-reading a complicated score of six sharps and trillions of semi-quavers, interspersed with some thumping jazz-rock chords for the high-kicking sections. Twenty enthusiastic pairs of legs lashed out in a brave attempt at unison as their amateur choreographer, a bossy redhead from Physiotherapy, took the ranks through a dance routine from *Beauty and the Beast*.

The choreographer came across to thank Hannah for filling the breach at such short notice. 'Fingers' Forsyth had been called to an emergency, but he'd be official pianist for this production. 'I hear you'd like to be up there with the chorus line,' she smiled, but we haven't yet cast the Good Fairy and we need a dancer with some background in classical ballet.'

'Disco dancing's more my thing,' explained Hannah. 'I did grade three ballet — when I was ten! What would I have to do?'

'You come on brandishing a sword, pirouetting round the Beast, hypnotising him with your speed and agility.

Then when he's helplessly transfixed, you slice off his head and out leaps this handsome Prince.'

Hannah privately thought this getting a bit far from the traditional version of *Beauty and the Beast* . . . for doesn't Beauty find the Beast dying for lack of her love? . . . but it certainly solved the transformation problem from beast to man. 'But,' pointed out Hannah with her usual concern for practicalities, 'how are you going to manage that? We haven't even got a proper stage, let alone a trapdoor.'

'We're getting a portable stage from one of the schools of drama, and a smoke device will provide cover to get the prince on stage.' The freckly physiotherapist was all brisk confidence. 'And if we could rely on you to help out with the piano when Dr Whatsisname's on call, it'd be absolutely super. Your sight-reading's first rate.

'Okay, everyone! Let's just run through that last number one more time, and then we'll call it a day. The principals want to come in here at nine sharp.'

Beauty, it transpired, was being played by a staff nurse from Paediatrics with the most amazing fall of corn-gold curls. She wasn't a quarter as glamorous as Mango, thought Hannah, asked to stay on at the piano for the rest of the evening. She wondered when she was expected to do her own audition for this ballet sequence, and knew she'd be far happier just kicking her heels up with the rest of the chorus line. She peered at the small group of shadowy figures standing further down the hall beyond the lighted area. It might be on the chilly side, but the place had proper blackout, and they ought to be able to squash in a few hundred at each of the two performances.

She peered at the music for Beauty's next song. Yes, she knew that one all right. It was lovely . . . Beauty had met this young man riding in the fields near her merchant father's home. The rider is wondrously handsome but quite ordinarily dressed, even shabby. Too shabby for her widowed father to welcome into their prosperous home.

There was a fair amount of muttering and movement from the dark areas of the hall during Beauty's song. The staff nurse's loosened hair shone like spun gold beneath the lights, and her rather sharp nose cast an unfortunate shadow over her upper lip giving her the appearance of an ill-tempered bird. However, her figure was without fault. Careful stage lighting and a deft stage make-up should take care of the visual problem.

'Very nice, darling.' Yet another unfamiliar voice echoed out of the darkness. Hannah swivelled on the piano stool, screwing up her eyes and trying to see who else was out there watching the singer. There seemed to be half a dozen 'directors' in this production.

'Just try and pitch your voice a shade higher, can you? Pianist, give her a strong lead — lovely, that's just the ticket. Off you go then, Beauty.'

Two verses later he interrupted again, whoever he was. This time his patience sounded taut. Again Hannah peered round. Of course it was impossible to know all the staff of a great teaching hospital: but there was something very familiar about the ring of this richly carrying voice. 'Listen to yourself, darling. You're still singing under the note.' The darlings were tripping off the tongue as if a chance to share in the direction had quite gone to this particular doctor's head. At least, supposed Hannah, puzzling out whom he might be, it was more than likely to be one of the medics. They were often musically talented or interested in dramatic productions, being clever and fond of the limelight.

'You're looking marvellous, honey. That hair is wonderful under the lights. Just relax and take it again now.'

But Beauty was beginning to fidget uncertainly, her stance tense and her hands clenched into fists. Hannah had the awful feeling the poor girl was working herself up to screaming point. Before even the first verse had finished, voices were talking across the singer down there in the murk. And Hannah's sensitive ears had picked up another deeply remembered sound. No question where that voice was concerned. Jon Harrington certainly had a facility for turning up when you were least expecting him, decided an incredulous Hannah; that devotion to his work could not be as ruthlessly single-minded as brother Sebastian had proclaimed, if Jon was inclined to take an interest in something as frivolous as a hospital panto, devoted to sending up senior staff in comic cameos with ribtickling glee. What a pity no one had suggested Jon Harrington audition for the Beast!

One moment Hannah had been playing without a trace of selfconsciousness, feeling herself as anonymous as a robot ordered to stop and start at the choreographer's whim. Next moment there was a tremble in her slender fingers and the awful realisation that her hair was freshly washed and unruly, her clothing chosen for an evening slumped at her desk, her face scrubbed and naked but for the trace of eyeliner without which she would have felt totally plain.

Everyone else's attention was on the singer in her lone spot beneath the centre light. But somewhere in the dark well of the hall stood Jonathan Harrington. And goodness knows how long he'd been out there listening to her playing. Hannah swallowed and her mouth grew dry with shame, as she imagined Jon's hawk eyes straying to the church mouse at the piano stool, the amusement on his craggy face as he noted the long legs in scarlet tights, the old grey skirt rucked thigh-high by the piano stool: Nurse Westcott dressed for an evening in the privacy of her little cubbyhole of a room.

Her shoulderblades contracted beneath the cherry wool sweater as she imagined those purple-grey eyes boring into her narrow, unprotected, and hitherto unsuspecting back.

Pull yourself together, Westcott! Hannah

scolded herself. You're hyperventilating! What do you want to do? Make yourself faint and really grab everyone's attention? I'm beginning to think you *have* got a crush on that beast out there . . . sorry, only joking, I know you don't *really* care about not being more elegantly dressed and not having bothered to blow-dry your hair to shiny smoothness. As if Dr Beast would actually bestir himself to notice! Anyway, Miss Church Mouse, how he chooses to spend his spare time is no fit topic for your speculation. So just fix your eyes on the music and get on with it.

When the singer ceased abruptly in shrill midstream, shoulders heaving with ominous emotion, Hannah was herself in such a state of mutual sympathy that she could have rushed to the girl and put a comforting arm about those quivering shoulders. But people were chatting and giggling most rudely and with no consideration for Beauty's feelings. It just made Hannah's blood boil. Imagine the courage it took to stand in front of everyone and open your mouth and . . . and *sing*. Didn't anyone have a heart out there? Where they all clones of Dr Harrington?

Indignation galvanised Hannah into action. She'd not have dared it for herself, but she never could bear to see another lack a champion. Shielding her eyes with both hands, she walked across to the front of the area designated 'stage'. 'Are you listening to me? This music is too high for her voice. Let's try again with it transposed to a lower key. B flat will suit her voice better.'

Someone sniggered and called back, 'Flat's about the right word!' but the mutter of conferring voices stilled to listen. Hannah waited impatiently, marvelling at the steadiness of her own words. The ensuing silence suggested they were thinking her suggestion over. But Beauty had other ideas.

'Don't bother!' she shrieked in best prima donna fashion, apparently ungrateful that Hannah was prepared to stand as her lone champion. 'Clearly I'm just not good enough. Go and find yourself another Beauty!' she hurled as a parting shot into the darkness. 'This panto stinks!' And with that their star was gone.

Hannah just stood there biting her lip while the slam of the door echoed in her shocked ears. Poor, poor thing! She bridled with indignation as guffaws of unchivalrous masculine laughter rent the darkness of the 'auditorium'. Jon Harrington's voice had a most uncharacteristic chuckle as Hannah heard him chiding another unseen companion with, 'Thought you'd come along to help, not hinder, Marcus old chap. At this rate you'll sabotage the whole damn show!'

There came a scratching of matches and a flare of phosphorus, and Hannah, lingering uncertainly in her patch of light, could smell the rich smoke of an expensive cigar and see the glow intensify as someone drew hard on best Havana. So much for Jonathan's lecture on the evils of smoking that day as she'd with foolish innocence let herself be charmed to the very edge of hero-worship as they chatted together by the swimming pool. But teetering on the brink of signing up as a life-member of the Jon Harrington fan club, she'd been saved by the skin of her teeth. With his own mouth, he had condemned himself as the heartless beast he truly was.

Just as Hannah turned to slip silently away, someone called out from the cluster of chorus girls who had stayed to watch the principals selected. 'Why doesn't Hannah Westcott audition for the lead? She can sing like a nightingale. We've heard her in the bath!'

'Hannah?' enquired that voice again that had Hannah so puzzled. It wasn't Jonathan this time, but another voice that somehow made her think of an actor playing Shakespeare — a voice trained to make the most of its natural gifts. A professional voice. Now who in the hospital would possess anything so distinctive . . . ? 'Hannah?' it said again. 'Who, pray, is Hannah?'

Just on the point of tiptoeing back

into the shadows to make her getaway, Hannah was trapped by a giant looming out of the darkness and grasping her by the arm, not especially gently. 'Here is Hannah,' announced Dr Harrington, and, 'Oh no, you don't,' he warned her, more forbiddingly heroic than ever in sleek black cords and a close-fitting black lambswool polo sweater. He swung her about and placed her unceremoniously centre-stage, stepping back and assessing her tight short skirt and red clinging jumper with all the subtlety of a radar scanner. The trouble, agonised Hannah, is that this terrible man notices everything about a person, down to the smallest detail. Her nails dug into damp, work-scoured palms as she made a determined effort to hang on to her nerve, then gasped in amazed disbelief as one of the world's most fêted actor-playwrights sauntered into the limelight to join them.

'Marcus Shero,' said Jonathan, with small necessity, for there was a general gasp from those not already in the know, and the whisper echoed throughout the chilly

reaches of the big hall. Marcus Shero!
Marcus *Shero* . . .

Hannah and Pete were two of his
greatest fans. They'd seen Shero's latest
black comedy, *Falling Slowly,* only the
week before she'd left for her holiday,
catching it just before the whole
production transferred to Broadway.

Hannah spoke — but no words came
out. She tried again. 'Marcus Shero — I
must be dreaming!'

Marcus seemed to find the spectacle
of the two of them highly entertaining
— his old Cambridge pal Jon, like a
powerful sleek black panther with its
quivering prey, a lissome figure in
scarlet and grey, the tumble of brown
hair gold-streaked beneath the lights.
Pretty oval face, dusted with freckles
but with a distinctively characterful
look about the girl's delicate aquiline
nose and stubbornly lifted chin. Now
this was the sort of mate for Jon. Far
more his type than Camilla with whom
he played a very dangerous game. Few
knew the truth behind that fascinating

affair: few other than Marcus himself. Even Sebastian was not entirely to be trusted with what had been going on between those two for well over a year.

Heartblock: it had long been Marcus Shero's diagnosis. But some day he'd discover the cure and reverse rôles with his good friend Jon to dispense a prescription.

He stretched out his hand and gripped Hannah's tight. 'This is Marcus Shero, believe you me. Flesh and blood. Take my pulse, little nurse, feel it beat.' He pressed the slim fingers around his wrist, clamped the cigar in his jaws and smiled down at Hannah, who was saying oh, my goodness and I just don't . . . lifting her head to seek the answer in Dr Harrington's watchful face.

They spoke across her, Marcus stooping to examine her face. He was stockily built, broad-shouldered but rather short in the leg, with the strong bold features that showed up so well on stage. He bought his clothes in New York, choosing distinctive jackets and bright shirts which he wore without ties. 'If you're going to be recognised everywhere you go,' he explained, 'you might as well give them something to look at!'

'Why's the kid so brown?' he wanted to know. 'It won't look right on the night if she isn't pale and pining.'

Hannah just looked from one to the other, bewildered by the sheer rapidity of events. 'Not to worry,' soothed Jon, 'she's just back from Spain, but it won't last five minutes in this climate. By Christmas I'll guarantee Hannah's white as a hospital sheet.' How did he know where she'd been? Was the whole world full of spies?

It quickly transpired that Jon had brought his old friend Shero to give the group of directors some professional tips. It wasn't feasible to depend on one person in the hospital situation, so several of the staff were sharing their time. Marcus Shero would come along whenever he could spare an evening — which wouldn't be too often. While he was explaining this in ringing tones to the hall at large, Hannah was obliged to stand there with Jon's hands pinioning her to one spot, the warmth and heaviness of his fingers seeming to melt the wool of her pullover and heat up the flesh and blood beneath. If the world could have frozen at that moment leaving the two of them transfixed in time, she would never weary of the sensation his touch now produced. So different from that dreadful morning in the lecture theatre . . . yet why?

Jon was still the same dominating, compelling, infuriating man. The kind of man Hannah never dared allow herself to dream about. Nothing had changed. No, she must learn her lesson from the past and stay resolutely wary . . .

'Right — let's get this show on the road,' ordered Marcus Shero, and Hannah remembered with a shudder how Jon had used the very same command at the start of his lecture. Jon felt the sudden shivery movement beneath his hands and took it for stage-fright. They hadn't given the poor child much choice in the matter; his fingers tightened their pressure, seeking to reassure. To Hannah it was a warning not to try and escape.

'If you sing as good as you look, darling, the lead is yours in my next Broadway transfer.' Marcus's encouraging wink was for her alone, and though Hannah knew well that this outrageous promise was to put her at her ease she goggled with brilliant-eyed wonder.

Jon was watching as the famous star took both her hands in his, mesmerising the girl into doing something that in her right mind she'd never have agreed to. He hoped Shero wasn't going to turn a young nurse's head; they hadn't even heard her sing yet!

Everything had happened too quickly for the dreaded nerves to shred Hannah's vocal chords to a tremble. It was Marcus Shero who, cigar clamped between his jaws, settled at the piano to accompany her. And Jon who merged panther-black with the shadows, to view her performance with critical ear and eye.

And all Hannah could think of as she

listened to those haunting opening bars was why, oh, why hadn't she brushed her hair properly and put on something a shade more dignified than her sister's cast-off grey mini-skirt?

4

Next morning Hannah overslept, leaping late out of bed and in a tizzy of excitement, all fingers and thumbs so that she laddered her black tights and spilled hairgrips on the crimson dhurri rug attempting to secure her silky mass of hair in a topknot. Such *news* she had to tell Pete! About her being thrust unwillingly into the lead rôle — yes, that, of course, but even more amazing about Jonathan Harrington and Marcus Shero appearing together in the Footlights productions at Cambridge University and remaining close friends ever since. That Shero had heard about the hospital's Christmas production from Jon, who was pumping him for ideas . . . got interested . . . and offered to come along — the famous *Shero!* — just for the fun of it.

Hannah struggled into her carefully

polished black lace-up shoes. They seemed a bit on the tight side this morning — perhaps success was going to her feet and not her head! To think of Jon cavorting on stage in the comic revues Footlights was so famed for, when she and Pete had quite decided there was not an ounce of humour in the Senior Registrar's autocratic he-man bulk. But at least she now understood why a man like Jon Harrington was getting actively involved in the hospital's panto.

As a rule Hannah dreaded the trapped sensation she got when riding the lifts. But today she was in a tearing hurry to catch Pete collecting the pre-breakfast lab samples of this and that on Grenville. By the time she reached the ward, however, there was no sign of the houseman.

He'd been on call, poor love, remembered Hannah guiltily. He'd be shattered, working through the night while she'd been basking in compliments and pats on the back — yes, literally, she could still feel the exact spot on her left shoulderblade where Jon's awesome hand had rested for a moment in congratulation of her performance.

'Well done, Hannah!' he'd said quietly. 'Marcus isn't easy to impress, but you've managed it. Don't go letting him steal you away to the London stage — we need bright young nurses like you.'

She'd been knocked speechless, her startled gaze lingering on Jon's broad back as he strolled away with Marcus Shero and out into the night.

Steady on, Westcott! Hannah hung up her cloak and quickly checked that her cap was holding fast to its newly-styled moorings. Don't go to extremes, will you! Don't start developing a *crush* on Dr Beast. Remember, no leopard ever changed its spots. He may well be the dishiest-looking doctor you've ever clapped eyes upon, but you know the score. Jonathan Harrington is wed to medicine and any nurse losing sleep over him is doomed to disappointment.

As usual the business of the day

claimed all concentration, and Hannah reverted to her usual down-to-earth self, making purposefully for the kitchen to start on breakfasts before the ward report at eight.

The night staff had forgotten to remove the eggs from the fridge for the second morning running. They were too cold for boiling and would crack in the egg pan. Hannah clicked her tongue. Rush, rush, rush — it was always the same. Half an hour to serve and clear away and be ready for Sister French.

*　*　*

Dr Fuller had enjoyed all of three hours' sleep. He came yawning into Grenville in search of Hannah. It was safe enough. Harrington and the big white chief wouldn't start their round before ten, and such busy men were seldom punctual. Just wait till she heard about Harrington's embargo on their relationship; knowing Hannah, she'd blow a fuse. The strong trampling on the weaker species, she'd say, imagined Pete with a grimace. It wasn't exactly flattering to himself — but pretty deadly accurate all the same.

There she was in the kitchen, bending over a pan of boiling water with a tablespoon in her right hand. God, she was a sight for sore eyes! The urgent business he'd come to relate went straight out of his mind, and tired as he was Pete succeeded in creeping in and making Hannah jump almost out of her lovely golden skin.

'I could have scalded myself!' Hannah's thoughts had been miles away. She frowned in reproof, her cheeks flushed and escaping tendrils of hair curling in the steam. 'Six soft-boiled . . . nine hard. Did you get any sleep last night, you poor man?'

'Not a wink,' lied Pete, making the most of her gentle concern, 'I could murder a coffee.'

Hannah fished out six eggs and gave Pete the spoon. 'Give the rest another couple of minutes while I make you a quick cup. The kettle's boiled.' She spun into action, already forgetting the extraordinary news she'd been longing to tell Pete.

'You've put your hair up. It suits you, Han, all swan neck and shell-like ears. You look like a convent school-girl.'

'Heaven forbid!' The trolley was stacked with plates of bread and butter and the big ward teapot. Hannah added the egg cups and whipped the rest of the eggs from the pan since Pete was too busy yawning to be any help.

Pete gulped his coffee down, and as Hannah was on the point of scurrying off to feed her patients he halted her in her tracks with an 'I've got some news for you. Interesting turn of events with Big Boy Harrington yesterday.'

Hannah glanced nervously across her shoulder to the empty corridor; the Registrar prowled as quietly as he spoke. She wished Pete wouldn't call him Big Boy — as if Jon was some bullying kind of prizefighter instead of clever . . . and subtle . . . and sophisti-cated. With a heart-stopping talent for inserting the knife where it would cause greatest anguish. Good grief, realised Hannah in wide-eyed surprise, I haven't thought of Dickie Derby in *days* . . .

'And I've got some news for you!' she began excitedly, but Pete was standing behind her, a hand squeezing her waist as he whispered into her exposed ear, 'Your infamous Dr Beast has forbidden me on pain of instant dismissal to come near you on this ward!'

On the trolley every cup rattled in outrage. 'He's *what?*' Hannah reacted with gratifying disbelief. 'I don't under-stand. Why should he?'

Pete pushed past her, shrugging wide but scrawny shoulders in a Gallic gesture of incomprehension. 'Guess he thinks my mind's more on you than my patients.'

'Oh, Pete, you must be careful. He doesn't know you very well yet. Hey, wait a moment — '

'Meet me in the canteen for lunch

and I'll tell you all about it. Must fly — that man-eating Sister Junor on Braybrooke will be waiting for me.'

Hannah pushed her trolley vigorously on to the ward, every movement reflecting righteous indignation. As if the two of them would be irresponsible enough for such reproof to be justified. Jon Harrington interfering in her personal life *yet again*. Another Dickie Derby episode! And to think that not eight hours ago he'd been positively tamed and amiable, joining in with the general agreement that she would be perfect for the lead in *Beauty and the Beast* and that she must let her hair grow at least until Christmas.

Hannah was strangely quiet as with Julie, the first-year nurse, and Nurse Li, a calm olive-skinned Malayan on her last ward before Finals, she dealt with the men's requirements. She'd been so embarrassed to find herself the focus of attention, hair awry in a tangled cloud, that skimpy little skirt and her legs all on show in blazing red tights that were fine for warmth in the privacy of one's room! And when she'd muttered something sheepish about hardly looking the part, Jon Harrington had regarded her with another of those quizzical stares and a sudden transforming smile that melted the last ounce of Hannah's determined resistance, so that she answered his own with a smile of unselfconscious happiness.

But her face had fallen the next instant.

'No problem,' he'd said, hooking his thumbs in his trouser pockets, lids drooping over the darkly penetrating eyes. 'The make-up department will transform you, Nurse Modesty, into a sensation.'

Hannah clattered dishes on to the trolley with unwonted fierceness. Of course he must have supposed she was fishing for compliments — and put her back in her place with the casual aplomb of the man of the world. Well, he wasn't so perfect himself. Had anyone ever told him there were definite bags under his eyes? How he'd acquired *those* was anybody's guess, and Hannah for one no longer cared to speculate on the Registrar and his love life.

'Sir Freddy's bi-weekly round today,' reminded Sister French. 'I know it isn't easy to make a men's ward look quite so homely as the likes of Braybrooke, but there's no excuse for any untidiness. Julie, keep yourself out of the way this morning. Your grandfather may well have the same symptoms as one of our patients, but Sir Freddy and Dr Harrington can diagnose perfectly well without your help. Staff will give you some jobs in the clean utility room to keep you busy.'

'Nurse Westcott, you're in charge of the records trolley this morning. And don't forget we've *two* Joneses this week — W. H. and J. P.'

A group of student doctors gathered outside the ward doors prompt at ten. Pete breezed in at ten past, thirty seconds ahead of the Chief and his retinue. He saw Hannah wheeling out the records trolley and came over. 'Now remember, Nurse, kindly refrain from your usual romantic behaviour. Call me 'doctor' if you have to speak to me in the course of your duties. Sounds better if you make it every other word — that way we'll have Harrington bemused and confused.'

'I don't think so, *Doctor*,' gritted Hannah out of closed lips. 'Take a look what's steaming up behind you.' The swish of white coats and tramp of advancing feet had Pete neatly side-stepping and taking his place at his Registrar's elbow. Hannah found her view of Dr Harrington's impressive profile decidedly uncomfortable and kept her eyes lowered to the manila folders in her care, steeling herself not to notice when Jon's fingers carelessly touched her outstretched hand as she gave and received back each file of patients' notes for Sir Freddy's inspection. Her spine was tense and her palms sweating at Jon's proximity, at watching and hearing him in quiet conference with Sir Freddy Blair and the senior members of the firm.

All was going well. Sir Freddy was an amiable man with greying hair worn rather long, and steel-framed bifocals settled upon a beaky fine-boned nose. His manner might be taken for that of an affable grandfather, but such paternalism hid a line of interrogation which kept the whole team on their toes, right down to a petite round-faced medical student who specially impressed Hannah with her readiness to speak up while her male colleagues shuffled in uncertainty over one of the chief's trickier questions.

The two senior physicians made a formidable pair. It was clear to Hannah, listening as intently as any, that neither would suffer fools gladly. They spoke to the anxious-eyed men, neatly tucked in their beds, with gentle consideration and painstaking explanations of their treatment. But any student who hadn't done his or her homework got very short shrift. Pete was scribbling like mad in his notebook as various tests were ordered.

There wasn't much drama about Sir Freddy's rounds. The cheerful greeting of each patient, the thoughtful conferrings out of earshot. 'Perhaps another blood count on the myeloid leukaemia . . . ' and, 'Our usual autumn influx of chest complaints, eh, Sister?' Polite requests for Dr Fuller to arrange another X-ray for Mr Hollis and further investigations to determine the efficiency of Mr Mason's kidneys.

By the end of the round all seemed to have gone well. Important clinical decisions had been calmly and unfussily made. Pete hadn't muffed anything and Hannah hadn't had any mishaps with the case notes. One of the medical students had been punctured with an icicle of chill sarcasm from Dr Harrington, but had asked for it, in Hannah's view, for he clearly hadn't read up one of the presenting cases.

Moreover, he'd pinched the bottom of the clever girl in full view of Dr Beast's eagle eye.

Hannah was walking up the corridor when the doctors emerged from drinking coffee in the office. She waited politely against the wall as they passed her by without a second glance, her eyes looking downward rather than at Jon Harrington, of whom she was intensely aware in his crisp white coat.

'Congratulations, Nurse!' she suddenly heard the deep voice murmur somewhere in the air above her head. 'Nurse Westcott is playing the lead in the hospital's pantomime this year, Sir Freddy. Excellent audition last night.'

The whole procession of doctors stopped and focused attention on Hannah. From the rear Pete reassured her with a huge wink and a grin. 'What are we doing this year?' enquired Sir Freddy. 'Not *Cinderella* again?'

The question was directed at Hannah, who blushed furiously and said, '*Beauty and the Beast,* sir,' wishing the ground would open up and swallow her for such presumption in taking on the glamorous lead.

'That's more original! Congratulations, Nurse, you'll make a charming heroine. Have we got a Beast?'

'Ye-es,' mouthed Pete, pointing a finger at Jonathan Harrington's impervious back. Hannah's lips twitched and were instantly controlled as she saw the Registrar frown and look round in the direction of her twinkling eyes.

'Of course, you're involved in this, aren't you, Jon? And we have the honour of your friend from Cambridge days, none other than Marcus Shero. I met a high court judge the other night who remembers seeing you in one of the Footlights revues that went up to the Edinburgh Festival. Any chance of you bringing Shero to supper with me and Dorothy? . . . rather a thrill to meet him.'

Pete's face was a picture. He looked as if he couldn't believe what he'd heard about his new boss Harrington. The man *was* human after all — and actually shared his and Hannah's fascination with theatricals. Wonders would never cease! And as for Hannah's snatching the lead rôle from beneath the noses of all those hopefuls who'd been trilling about their chances for weeks . . . so *that* was the news she'd spoken of when he'd been half awake. She'd be shocked when she heard the full facts about Harrington's embargo on their friendship. Shocked — and, knowing Hannah, defiant.

At midday they snatched ten minutes together in the canteen. The catering manager was making a valiant effort to alter the eating habits of patients and staff alike, by introducing a range of high-fibre low-fat dishes on to the menu. Pete had almost finished his lentil curry by the time Hannah arrived, plonked herself into a seat and dived into her chilli bean casserole.

'I hung on for you,' he pointed out, yawning. 'Then I'm off to my lonely bed. Wish you'd come with me, sweetheart.'

'Change the record,' said Hannah blandly. 'Was that stuff good? I nearly had some, but the chilli was too tempting. Mmmm, delicious! Now, I want to hear word for word what Dr Beast actually said . . . '

* * *

Mango was disappointingly unshocked. As she pointed out, 'Pete has this breezy slapdash manner which, while it's very goodhumoured and does wonders in relaxing the patients, is *bound* to get up the nose of a perfectionist like Jon Harrington. Besides, how do you know he's not exaggerating things to gain your sympathy? You know what a sucker you are, Hannah, for a hard luck story. He's hoping you'll kiss him better.'

Hannah's shoulders sagged as she recognised the sense of Mango's interpretation of events.

'Anyway, if you two go canoodling in the linen cupboard, what do you expect?'

'Mango! You've been reading too many romances. What do you take me for? You know I'd never go out of my way to encourage Pete and his fantasies about the two of us. In my book we're just comfortable friends who like going to the theatre together. I don't want emotional ties with any man. Not ever again. Well, not for years.'

'Peace, friend! I'm just giving you my opinion since you asked for it. Think about it. It's Harrington's job to train his junior doctors — and he clearly wants them all in the Harrington mould. Without any discernible human frailty. Now get your skates on and come for a drink. The whole crowd are waiting for us and it's after nine.'

'Who was that girl Sebastian mentioned?' questioned Hannah as they hurried along the lamplit streets. 'Camilla?'

'If you read *Vogue* you wouldn't have to ask that. Top model — Paris collections. Does a lot of photographic work in New York.'

'I supposed she was married to Jon when I first heard her name,' admitted Hannah in a small and chastened voice as her castles in the air crashed about her ears. 'That is — till I heard he wasn't the marrying kind, because of what happened between his parents in the past. He must have been terribly badly hurt.'

'It'll hurt his career if he doesn't find a wife some day,' pointed out Mango. 'The powers-that-be prefer consultants to be married. I guess Jon and Camilla *will* take the plunge one of these fine days. After all, even after two years they're still together.'

'You mean they live together?'

Mango laughed at the expression on Hannah's face as they passed under a street light. 'I wouldn't know,' she teased. 'But even if they do, I don't imagine they see overmuch of each other. You must be smitten, Hannie love. Is darling Jon *so* devastating in his white coat, then? He's certainly a sight for sore eyes out of his clothes — and we should know, shouldn't we!'

Mumbling protests, Hannah tramped after Mango into the smoky interior of the Lamb and Flag, and was instantly swallowed up in the camaraderie of hospital staff released from their working confines.

Pete had risen from his bed to join the jocular throng. He waved to Hannah and Mango as they appeared in the doorway and they came smiling over to join in the conversation. 'And I tell you she's not that bad-looking when she smiles,' Pete was insisting.

'I don't think I've ever had the privilege,' grimaced the SHO on the same firm, a Welshman with a yen for Mango.

'Doesn't make the most of herself — pasty skin, horrible hair.'

Hannah winced. 'Whoever are you lot dissecting now?'

'Your friend, beloved,' grinned Pete, slipping his free hand about Hannah's waist and waving a pint of bitter in the other so vigorously that everyone protested and moved back. 'Marta the Mamba. Has her knife into you, doesn't she, Han? You'll have to watch her, working on the same ward.'

'Marta's okay,' said Hannah uninterestedly, her eyes automatically checking the place for a certain figure who of late was dominating her life. She had never let on to Pete about that holiday in the South of France. He'd no idea she and Mango and his Senior Registrar had met in more . . . Hannah's throat tightened . . . intimate circumstances. She was so unsure of her own motives in keeping Pete in the dark about her past love-life — Dickie Derby and all that unhappiness. Water under the bridge. She'd grown a lot older and wiser since then. Wiser! That was a laugh, she mused, acknowledging her sense of disappointment at failing to pick out the man her eyes, with a will of their own, searched for.

Mango was stringing Pete along, apparently drinking in his tales of woe about the rough treatment his Senior Registrar was meting out, winking at the Welshman as he lit her cigarette for her. 'Challenge Dr Harrington to pistols at dawn in Hyde Park!' she suggested naughtily.

'Futile, my dear Watson,' declaimed Pete in ringing tones. 'That man is fire- and bullet-proof . . . you've got to admire his style, though. Never raises his voice as he deals out the heavy sarcasm. And it's beastly effective — makes a guy feel about six inches high.'

Hannah wished Pete wouldn't shout so. She pressed her hands to her ears as the clatter of voices threatened to engulf her, cursing under her breath as the sleeve of her tartan shirt trailed in a puddle of beer. She rolled the long sleeves up, displaying smooth skin still bearing traces of suntan, quite unaware of the eyecatching picture she made in her tight jeans and brushed cotton shirt with its red and blue and green tartan, her hair loose and fluffy about her flushed, anxious face.

'I admire the guy, really and truly, deep down,' Pete was telling his interested audience. 'His standards are just way beyond my reach. But if I'm honest, Harrington's the sort of doctor I want to be when I grow up!' Pete guffawed at the effect of his own wit which had the others groaning. 'Every night I'm going to write out a hundred lines: I must try to please Big Boy Harrington, I must try to please Big Boy Harrington, I must — '

Hannah had to raise her own voice to be heard above the din. Anything to divert the subject away from this uncomfortable track. 'We've all heard enough, thank you, Pete. Let us now conclude the saga of Jonathan Harrington's persecution of his house physicians. Amen.' Pete had grabbed her hand and was squeezing it rather painfully, a strange expression on his long face as he seemed to signal messages with his eyebrows.

Hannah frowned. 'Now what's the matter with you?' she queried exasperatedly.

'Good evening,' said a deep voice from behind her. 'Dr Fuller — Nurse Westcott.'

'Evening, sir,' muttered Pete.

146

Hannah felt a wave of chill as the black shadow passed between her and the light. 'Evening, Dr Harrington,' murmured other voices, breaking once more into chatter as Jon pushed his way through the crowd to where other senior doctors had gathered in the well of the room. Because of its proximity to the hospital the Lamb and Flag was a popular venue with all the medical and nursing staff. Their bar snacks were excellent too.

'I'm hungry,' declared Pete, not particularly nonplussed by Dr Harrington's untimely appearance. 'Want a toasted sandwich, love?'

The very thought turned Hannah's stomach. 'Pete! Am I an idiot! He *must* have overheard.'

'So what?' Pete stood up and placed his hands firmly on her shoulders. 'Now I'm going to order toasted cheese and ham. Are you about to change your mind and have some too?'

'I couldn't eat a thing.'

'*What* did I hear you say?' Mango

disentangled herself from the clutches of the rugger-playing SHO, who was tackling her with more enthusiasm than finesse. 'Get off, you Welsh thug, you, and allow me to speak to my friend. Pete — what have you done to our Hannah? She eats like a horse, unless she's in love.'

'You mean I've cracked it at long last?' roared Pete, increasing his grip on Hannah's shoulders and posturing with an extravagance that had his onlookers guffawing encouragingly. 'She loves me! Did you hear that, everyone? She loves me!'

Afterwards Hannah was to wonder if she would have reacted as she did if Dr Harrington had not so obviously been watching Pete's raucous display. It was like a re-run of that afternoon in Provence, Jon leaning on the door of his sports car, cold-eyed and appraising; contemptuous of the antics of even his own brother cavorting noisily with an underclad female of the rich and spoiled variety.

And here was Pete making a deliberate exhibition of himself and involving the unwilling Hannah as his stooge and partner in a specially embarrassing way. But short of standing on the table and announcing, 'I do not love this fathead! but he's a very kind and caring person and you're all seeing the worst side of him — ' Hannah could only ride things out with a goodhumoured shudder at such clowning. And then make a run for it.

Pete, of all people, knew her feelings for him. And they did not include love.

'I'm going back,' she whispered to Mango when Dr Fuller had gone to order his sandwiches. 'Don't let him come after me, *please*, Mango. I've had as much Pete as I can swallow for tonight.'

Mango nodded with a grim smile. 'Thought you might have. I say, I wonder why Jon Harrington keeps staring at you? Have you noticed? I have a shrewd suspicion that seeing us both together has triggered off some interesting thoughts.'

That did the trick. Hannah was out

of the Lamb and Flag before anyone could guess her intention. The streets were well lit, there were still plenty of folk strolling about or hurrying homeward. And though wandering in the dark was not something she chose to do often, Hannah struck off in the opposite direction to the Royal Hanoverian's comforting presence, turning up the collar of her navy jacket to hide her hair and thrusting her hands deep into capacious pockets. It was a mild damp night for November, with smudgy starless skies.

The first year had been the worst. But it was true — you did get over things. Hearts were tougher than one might guess at the time. And without the aide-mémoire of his photograph, Dickie's face was actually rather difficult to recall. Too smoothly handsome, without any endearing flaw to jog the memory. Now Pete — you could describe his looks as a collection of endearing flaws. That boyish smile revealing one hooked eye-tooth; that long-chinned face; the mobile eyebrows which punctuated his jokes.

No, there was no serious romance in her life now.

Hannah sighed heavily; if she could rid herself of this peculiar fascination with Jon Harrington then life would flow back into its normal channels. But things hadn't been the same since the discovery that he was here, working within the environs of the Hanoverian. A man she had several excellent reasons to dislike.

Shivering, she glanced up at the dark plum skies, an awareness growing that the street, so silent and empty, now echoed to the tread of another's footsteps. And yes, they were pacing along behind her, deliberately matching their strides to her smaller, shorter ones, seeking neither to catch her up or overtake.

An icy fear traced the channel of Hannah's spine and the back of her neck prickled with tension. She fought to keep her wits under control. Should she stop and pretend a stone was in her shoe, like they did on TV? See if the steps slowed to a halt . . .

Or should she make a run for it? A headlong dash into the night towards the refuge of the Hanoverian . . .

What if she should turn about, face her unseen shadow!

Hannah drew a trembling, shallow breath, and turned. To meet whatever threatened.

5

Though a headmistress of the old brigade, Miss Wilson believed in preparing her 'gels' for anything; and her eyes were wide open to the sort of hazards the High School pupils might come up against as they strode confidently through life. Every pupil, therefore, learned from experts in the art of self-defence how to look after herself if threatened with Actual Bodily Harm: no punches pulled, no blushes spared, kick 'em where it hurts, young ladies. And full marks if they're stretcher cases afterwards. It's simply a matter of technique.

Good old Miss Wilson.

Hannah filled her lungs and expelled all her terror in a wild howl of aggression, just as she'd been taught.

'No-o-o!'

And sure enough it wrong-footed her assailant.

She'd reached a pool of lamplight, half expecting to find it was Pete tracking her through the deserted streets. But the glaring eyes of a stranger, dirty football scarf muffling the lower half of his face, met hers as she swung to confront him, fastening upon the girl with impersonal malevolence.

The man had probably been anticipating a thin scream of fright. Puzzlement flickered in those slitted eyes — a second's hesitation over Hannah's throaty shout which warned, 'Back off! I intend to defend myself.'

But still the man came on. Keep thinking keep thinking *keep thinking*! A surge of anger and adrenalin galvanised Hannah. Not a schoolgirl 'opponent' this time, the pair of them gigglingly reluctant to hurt each other, but another living being intent on imposing his will upon hers by sheer brute strength.

Hannah went forward, furious with terror and rage, her mind weirdly detached and dishing out instructions as coolly as if listing the steps of a recipe. Grind your heel into his shins. Swing your arms together and up and break the lunge of his outstretched hands. Great stuff! You've got him at a disadvantage, so strike at that exposed throat with the side of your hand. Fingers jabbing at his eyes and twisting his nasty nose. Elbow sharp and bony striking into his solar plexus.

The air was full of their furious struggle, but amazingly it was Hannah on the attack, he striving to cover his own vulnerability, wondering what the hell he'd come up against, gasping and cursing as he fought off this hellcat. And it was he who lost his footing first as Hannah swung her whole weight on the throttling football scarf, choking and gurgling and striking his head with a sickening crack against the lamp-post as he went down.

Hannah's immediate reaction was disastrous. In a grossly ill-timed sense of duty she bent down to her assailant in horrified concern. And two violent evil-smelling hands closed upon her throat . . .

Now there was every reason to kill her. But it wasn't going to be quick. A cruel hand wound into the softness of her hair, a fist smashed into her face . . . Hannah saw stars.

Neither had been aware of the car screaming to a halt, slewed across the road, headlights outlining the struggle in full beam. 'You filthy brute!' bellowed a hostile voice, and next moment Hannah's assailant was on his feet and making off with a dragging, limping run which suggested he was not feeling as well as he might have expected, considering his chosen victim was a slip of a female.

Another pair of male hands was upon her now, lifting her to her feet, all strength and concern and kindness, then seeing how she swayed dizzily with the metallic taste of blood seeping down her throat and trickling thickly from one nostril, bearing her like some precious parcel to the car — engine still running — and stowing her carefully beneath a warm fringed rug on the back seat. 'I — I'm perfectly all right,' claimed Hannah weakly. 'You should have seen the one that got away!'

'I know,' said Dr Harrington, for it was none other, 'I had a ringside view. If the guy's got any sense he'll be heading for Casualty. Just as we are.' He ignored the feeble protests from the back seat and in moments they were parked outside the emergency bay and Jonathan was sweeping her up in his arms once more and elbowing aside the swing doors of the department.

Casualty was quiet, the late-night brawlers yet to come or already dealt with. The staff nurse recognised Dr Harrington immediately and, on being told the patient was a nurse, set the VIP treatment in action. She herself manned the treatment room and helped Hannah out of her ripped jacket and filthy clothes. She hesitated before tackling the skin-tight muddied jeans. 'You weren't stabbed?' she questioned. 'You're absolutely sure? We've seen cases where tight denims were acting as tourniquets for a haemorrhage — blood gushing everywhere when we undressed the patient — who practically exsanguinated on the spot.'

'I guess I was lucky,' said Hannah weakly. 'My attacker didn't seem to be carrying a knife. He must have thought I'd be easy prey without!'

The staff nurse smiled grimly. 'I hear you gave him a rough time. Bully for you! I'm none too happy myself, coming on duty after dark.'

The jeans were off, and the shirt. Hannah sat on the treatment couch having her bruised face swabbed and feeling every inch of her had been trampled by a rhinoceros. She was still wearing her red ankle socks and her bra and pants, streaks of dirt across her face and forehead and her hands scratched and filthy. Jon Harrington came in, closely followed by the duty casualty officer. Hannah felt too wounded to care what they thought of her bizarre appearance. Jon Harrington had seen it all before anyway. In France, if he did but know it, and that other week in Lecture Theatre 3.

They told her to lie flat and she complied. She hadn't been aware of pain at any time during the attack — until her hair was grabbed. Now it all hurt, from her swollen scalp to her hammering toes.

The two doctors were kind and gentle and very, very thorough. They watched her face to gauge her emotions, told Hannah she was incredibly brave to defend herself like that, asked where she'd picked up such a technique, and applauded all enlightened headmistresses.

'You say the feller cracked his head on the lamp-post,' noted the casualty officer, Dan Hardy. 'We'll be keeping a weather eye out for that one.' He washed his hands and dried them on a paper towel, interestedly observing the dishevelled student nurse with her tangled mass of bronzey hair, shell-shocked eyes and pretty pouting mouth. At least he'd hazard a guess it would be pretty when the swelling had gone down and that raw split had healed. As for the nose . . .

'Better get you down to X-Ray. What do you think of the nose, Jon?'

Jon Harrington was regarding the nose, arms folded, head tilted at a quizzical angle. He reached out and grasped Hannah's chin, and the touch of his fingers on her face made her suddenly begin to tremble. 'It's all right,' he said considerately, misinterpreting her reaction, 'you've had a nightmare of an experience, but it's over now.'

To her chagrin Hannah felt her eyes fill with foolish tears. If Jon hadn't by the grace of fortune arrived in the nick of time, there was no telling what the outcome might have been. She wanted to thank him, but couldn't trust herself to speak without crying buckets and making an utter idiot of herself.

'We-ell,' he was opining slowly, 'they never did anything about my nose when I broke it on the rugby field . . . '

'But you ain't as beautiful as she is, pal.'

'True. True.'

They were teasing her, trying to keep her spirits up. Hannah smiled dutifully through the livid bruising.

The doctors were closely regarding her face, checking left and right profiles and gently probing the swollen tissues. 'Nice tan,' said Dan. 'Where've you been, South of France?'

Hannah went rigid! She mumbled something through cracked lips, but Jon didn't appear to be especially interested in either question or answer, concentrating on the immediacy of her injuries. 'I think we should admit her for a couple of days just to be on the safe side. Don't you agree, Dan? We've a bed on Braybrooke. I'd prefer to keep this young lady under observation myself.'

Hannah couldn't control a heartfelt groan.

'You lucky girl,' said Dan, giving the registrar a wink and an aye-aye, I don't blame you, nod of agreement. After an experience such as she'd gone through,

Hannah Westcott would certainly bene-fit from some considerate doctoring if she wasn't going to end up on a psychiatrist's couch. Reaction was often delayed in these cases and could result in a girl being too traumatised to go anywhere on her own again. Fortunately she'd protected herself pretty effectively from actual rape. Having a guy like Jon Harrington taking a personal interest in her recovery was all to the good. That's what Dan had meant by 'lucky girl'.

Hannah, however, heard him, and her blood ran hot and cold. Didn't the casualty officer realise it had just been force of circumstance that brought Dr Harrington driving along that particular street on his usual route home? That any interest the Medical Registrar had was the strictly impersonal concern of the doctor for a newly admitted patient?

The knowledge that she was, too, a patient impinged on Hannah's awkward embarrassment. Used to being the nurse, she now must submit to being looked after. The prospect held little appeal, but with any luck it would only be for twenty-four hours . . .

So, X-rays and a warm bath later found Hannah tucked up in the side ward of Braybrooke — directly across the way from Grenville where, unsuspecting, she had spent the working day. Sometimes it was brought home to you in a very peculiar way that it was a good thing you couldn't see into the future. Who could have guessed, she mused dopily, that tomorrow Mango would be nursing *her* of all people? Or that she'd be Pete and Jonathan's patient that very night.

The night staff were enjoying having a rather uninteresting spell of duty interrupted by the novelty of a Hanoverian nurse being admitted in fairly dramatic circumstances; plus the added excitement of Dr Harrington looking in with welcome frequency, in addition to his normal round. Though they *were* getting used to the fact that he was one of those doctors who might appear at any hour of the day or night if a particular case was causing him concern. It certainly added a frisson to the long nights — for he was a heartbreaker all right. Nurse Wiseman reckoned she'd used up two tubes of Bronze Lamé lipstick since Dr Harrington had joined the staff. Not to mention the amount of blusher it took to keep at bay the pale and uninteresting look you tended to get working nights.

'You still awake?' she said, flashing her torch on to the ceiling of Hannah's side room. Nurses were always given a room to themselves if at all possible.

'I keep yawning, but I can't seem to drop off. My mind won't stop thinking.'

'Are you comfortable, love? Any more pain?'

Hannah moved her head heavily on the pillow. Dr Harrington himself had slid the analgesics painlessly into her system with a deft needle. 'It's just the strangeness of it all. Being here instead of in my own bed, wearing this hospital nightie.' Mentally kicking myself for being so idiotic as to roam about the city streets on my own, she might have added.

'It's understandable — after what you've been through.' The night nurse was curious to find out more. A cup of tea would be nice; the two of them could have a chat while her colleague kept an eye on the big ward. 'I'm going to brew up,' she said. 'I'll bet you could do with a hot, strong cuppa.'

'And so could I, Nurse!' added a deep voice from out in the corridor. Hannah's rescuer loomed hugely in the doorway, a black silhouette, shoulders like an ox — Pete had said — built like a side of beef. How effective would schoolgirl self-defence be against *that* mighty physique? Hannah swallowed dryly and shuddered. 'Thank you.' Her voice was a mere whisper. 'Some tea would be nice.'

Wiseman beamed. 'There's a sliced lemon in the fridge for you, Dr Harrington. I wrapped it in cling-film to keep it nice and fresh.' She remembered Hannah.

'Don't take sugar, do you, dear?'

'Just one — if it's no trouble. I don't want to be a nuisance.' But I am, of course I am! Struggling weakly against emotion mingled with fury at her own foolishness, Hannah blinked away the tears that had dissolved Dr Harrington into a wavering black nightmare moving closer to her bed.

'How is my patient?' he was asking as the night nurse glided past him to the door, intent on filling the kettle and glossing her lips.

'Wide awake, as you see. She can't stop thinking, can you, dear? Let's pop the light on so Doctor can have a little look.' Nurse Wiseman came back and flicked the switch of the night light over the bed, then went on her way. Hannah wished people would stop talking to her as if she was a halfwit, and wondered if she was guilty of that herself. How carefully she would listen to the way she spoke to patients in the future! She bore Jon's intent regard with a certain tension, her battered face shuddering

166

beneath the path of his eyes as they traced the course of her injuries.

Then the fingers took over, infinitely careful, cool as the snows of Everest, yet making her flesh burn and pulsate as the shape of bone was traced and explored, the eye-socket outlined, and the delicate aquiline nose.

To think she of all people was now Jon Harrington's patient. 'Will I live?' questioned Hannah, trying to make light of a situation she found well-nigh unbearable. Any doctor but this one . . . any! Where Jon Harrington was concerned she was all confusion. Yet only weeks ago (you could measure the time in days!) her feelings towards Jonathan Boyd-Harrington had been perfectly straightforward, thank you. Or rather no, thank you. He was not to be trusted, never to be forgiven. And never, she had innocently believed, never to be encountered again, for they moved in completely separate worlds.

Yet here *was* Jonathan Harrington, MRCP. Most decidedly taking her under his wing, and displaying qualities she would once have sworn under oath to be totally alien to his character, demonstrating such reassuring confidence and empathy that Hannah was beginning to realise it was foolish to keep up all this reserve and suspicion. Just relax, her befuddled mind was insisting, Dr. Harrington knows best, he understands what you've been through, he'll look after you now. Didn't he, after all, save your life tonight?

Hannah looked directly into those purple-grey eyes so thoughtfully examining hers. I chose to dislike this man more than anyone else in the world. I nicknamed him Dr Beast. He ruined my love life. And he's the man who saved me . . .

He was smiling, and it was devastating. Hannah fell in love at that very moment. Her heart soared into her eyes. But for the fact that they were puffed and swollen to mere slits, Jon would have seen it all. He simply saw that she was struggling to find words of gratitude, and hastily he forestalled this as the painful lips parted and the newly scabbed injury threatened with fresh pearls of bright red blood.

'No problems. No bony injuries on your X-rays. But you can't go back on Grenville for a week — the sight of you's enough to scare the crows!'

Hannah's crystallising love dissolved on the instant. Thank you very much! That demonstrated how far you could trust a Beast! His less endearing side was never far from the surface. The greeny eyes darkened with pain, but again the swelling prevented Jon from reading the message in her expression.

'I'll keep you in here for twenty-four hours' observation, then off you go home to Mummy and Daddy to be made a fuss of.'

'But I've only just started on Grenville,' wailed Hannah without moving her lips. In came the night nurse with the tea.

'Can't be helped,' said the Registrar, so unsympathetically that Hannah was by now convinced it was all truly a nightmare. 'I'll take mine in the office, thanks. I want to write up Nurse Westcott for some more medication. Can't have her lying there thinking all night, can we, Nurse?' and Hannah was left with her tea and her seething emotions as their footsteps moved softly away.

'He can't *wait* to be rid of me, that's what!' she told herself, jumping to a conclusion that Jon Harrington could hardly have foreseen and would have ridiculed as typical of female logic. 'All right then, I'll go, since I'm obviously — and, I can promise you, *unwillingly* — taking up one of Sir Freddy's precious beds.'

For the next five minutes Hannah lay and fumed alone in the darkness till Nurse Wiseman returned with a pill that knocked her straight into the realms of oblivion. Considerately, no one disturbed her until Pete turned up to do the pre-breakfast tests and shake her awake with an exasperated hand.

He was full of questions which demanded and accused. But Hannah's mouth was even worse, the lips gummed together with dried blood, cracked, dry and peeling. 'God, you look terrible,' he said, but coming from Pete it didn't somehow have the same impact. Something to do with Hannah feeling she didn't much care if Pete saw her looking her worst. But with Jon Harrington . . . well, she had to show herself to be other than the little church mouse he'd described her as in France.

'What an idiotic thing to do, running off like that!' Pete was pacing up and down, raking his hair with outraged fingers till it stood on end like Strewelpeter's. 'You of all people, Hannah. You're supposed to be so *sensible*. D'you realise you gave me one hell of a fright? . . . Do you?'

'S-sorry, Pete,' whispered Hannah meekly, quite enjoying the spectacle of the young houseman's concern. It was a pretty fair take-off of the lead character in the play they'd seen last at the

National. She hoped Pete wouldn't forget his audition for the panto on Friday night. The panto! Rehearsals would be out for a week or so, now she was in this state.

'Harrington's got hold of the idea it was *me* drove you into the arms of that rapist!' Pete saw the question in Hannah's eye and shook his head. 'No, they haven't managed to catch the bastard. Here, try and sip some more water. I'll support your head. Oh God, Han, I can hardly bear to look at what that devil's done to you!'

'Perhaps I'd better . . . audition . . . for the Beast!' croaked Hannah, smiling at Pete with eyes that were mere slits between swollen eyelids.

He had the grace to wince. 'And speaking of Dr Beast, hear this. He wouldn't let me see you when you were admitted — said he considered I'd upset you quite enough for the time being, and you were not, repeat not, to be disturbed.' Hannah tried to interject a whispered, 'But he did save my life,

172

actually, Pete,' but she couldn't stem the flow of the young houseman's hurt and indignation. 'I ask myself, what did I do except turn my back for thirty seconds — during which you vanished into thin air. Mango made out she knew nothing about it. I supposed you must have gone off to the ladies', or of course I'd have come looking for you.'

Hannah patted his hand. 'Just wanted . . . breath of fresh air. I'll explain to Jo- . . . to Dr Harrington . . . when it's less painful to speak.' Gingerly her fingers probed her bruised and swollen larynx, so violently throttled by those horrid, evil-smelling hands. Brrr! shivered Hannah, pulling the sheet right up to her chin.

'He wants to cause trouble between you and me,' Pete was vowing with dark melodrama. 'He fancies you, Hannah. Wants you for himself.'

Water spluttered over her pillow and Hannah dabbed at her sore mouth with the back of her hand. Whatever would that idiot come up with next? 'What rot!' If only it were true . . .

When Mango came on duty, for Braybrooke was her own ward, it was VIP treatment for the rest of the day. Sister Junor paid a couple of perfunctory visits, but clearly regarded nurse-patients as something of a nuisance. And thanks to her prescribed medication Hannah slept heavily throughout the night, quite oblivious of the visit of the tall, dark doctor who stood silently at her bedside for several minutes during the small hours.

* * *

Jon Harrington rubbed the back of his neck and eased the tension in his shoulders. It was all very well being taller than most men, but he hadn't played squash for over a fortnight and the lack of exercise made bending over patients and pen-pushing at desks take its toll on his spine. He reached for the last folder and stared at the name on the cover. Hannah Westcott. There was one lucky young lady.

The notes were brief and to the point, stating reason for admission and prescribed treatment. A minor condition, ready now for discharge. Jon Harrington's strong black scrawl added the one terse sentence. He snapped the cap back on his pen and tucked it into his breast pocket, clasping both hands behind his neck in an attitude of silent contemplation, eyes half closed, lower lip out-thrust. He had never believed, he reminded himself, that there was much to be gained from slotting people into categories. Take Nurse Westcott, as capable and sensible a nurse as you could ever hope to encounter. But she goes and does something so completely out of character as to make the mind boggle, and ends up battered and bruised in a hospital bed. Glib assumptions about another's character — that never worked. They'd turn around and surprise you the next moment.

Reflectively, Jon lowered his arms and began to trace the aggressive contours of his nose with an idle forefinger. He'd never fancied psychiatry as a career. And even appearances could prove quite remarkably deceptive. She might look the soft and gentle type, but by hell, she'd been fighting like a wildcat when he'd come upon that violent scene. No doubt about it, Hannah Westcott was not short of guts.

Jon's right hand checked the angle of his bow-tie. He wore it, not as an affectation, but because his father had always worn bow-ties. It was a link between them, even though the father was long dead, a mark of respect that looked beyond the alcohol and the womanising to bonds of blood and affection. If ever I have a son, mused Jon, ours will be a very different sort of relationship.

For no reason he found himself picturing Hannah that fateful night in the Lamb and Flag. In the set of her white, frozen face he had read trouble; and followed a discreet five minutes later, without a clue as to the direction of her flight, only by pure lucky fluke tracking her down. And in the nick of time.

Time! Jon glanced at his watch. Camilla's flight should be in. He must ring the flat. A whole month since she'd been in town, and he needed to know just what had happened out there in the Big Apple. Had she changed her mind after all about their . . . arrangement? Or was everything to carry on as before? He'd give her half an hour, then phone.

Jon strode along the corridor to Hannah's room, greeted her briefly and examined her injuries with fingers as cool as his manner. She thought he seemed remote this morning. Or perhaps not so much remote as considering in his mind weightier matters than her trivial case presented. But at least he seemed satisfied with her progress. 'Providing you promise to go straight home, and stay there for one whole week,' he warned, his eyes severe and watchful, 'I'm ready to discharge you. Forget the rehearsal schedule — I may be able to arrange one or two private sessions to help you catch up.'

'Th-thank you!' gasped Hannah, praying inwardly that Jon's examination would not be over-thorough and that she would not be obliged to submit her pounding heart to his stethoscope. Either the game would be up . . . or he'd assume she'd had a setback, and keep her stuck in that bed till kingdom come.

'What were you doing, then, roaming deserted London streets at that hour? I'd like to think there could be a rational explanation for such foolhardiness.'

Foolhardiness! How pompous Jon could be . . . deliberately Hannah kept her eyes on the green coverlet and a mutinous silence on her lips. As if she needed reminding how he had witnessed Pete Fuller's display of joie de vivre.

'A lovers' tiff?' suggested Jon amiably, settling himself on the chair by the window and stretching out the powerful length of his legs as if he had all the time in the world to await Hannah's response. Her sidelong glance took in the crisp cotton of his white shirt, its fine grey stripe complementing the immaculate cut of the charcoal grey suit jacket discarded for the usual white medical coat. Today, she observed with grudging admiration, the silken bow tie was a raffishly elegant shade of palest pink. Ever the impressive and high-powered doctor, stethoscope trailing nonchalantly from one pocket, that armful of folders tossed on top of her bed table, ready to be scooped up as Jon Harrington went on his way. The hapless Dr Fuller had forgotten just such a pile of patients' notes that very morning; and if Hannah hadn't called him back, almost tearing open her poor throat in doing so, it would have been the high jump for Pete from his lord and master here.

Knowing she should be genuinely grateful brought out the stubborn streak in Hannah's nature. For if Jon

Harrington had not been there in the Lamb and Flag, avidly observing that display of Pete's adoration, she'd never have left the pub on her own. So, if Jon did but know it, he was as culpable as Dr Fuller. And because it was impossible to tell him so, Hannah was less than polite. 'No!' she retorted to that impertinent question, examining the nails of her right hand and discovering that, short as they were, two had been broken in the desperation of her struggle.

'When I found you, you were nowhere near the hospital,' Jon was observing pleasantly, never once taking his eyes off Hannah's uncomfortable person. 'I noticed you left us all in something of a hurry.'

Us! Indignation was written all over his patient's delightfully expressive face; even the bruised swellings did not serve to disguise her feelings. A grin illuminated the doctor's mouth and eyes, and seeing it Hannah was both charmed and enraged — trapped there in that wretched bed, like a mouse, while the cat teased and protracted its merciless torture.

'Were you really on your way home?' she asked suddenly with a bold stare that took on the whole impact of those unfazed purple-grey eyes.

'No,' agreed Jon. 'I came looking for you. It's that face of yours. I can read exactly what's going through your fertile imagination. You were wild about something, and I didn't get the impression you were heading back to the Nurses' Home. As luck would have it, I managed to track you down, and — well . . . ' he shrugged expressively, lifting the breadth of his shoulders and then relaxing back against the too-small easy chair.

Fertile imagination! That face of yours! Hannah was so taken aback that her fabled way with words dried up like a well in a desert. 'Why should you of *all* people suddenly feel concern for my welfare?' Hostility blazed from between those swollen eyelids and her knuckles whitened as both hands gripped the sheets.

It was Jon's turn to frown in puzzlement. You of all people? Whatever was that supposed to mean? His mobile brow scarred with thought as his inner vision scanned his own conscience and came to a halt, baffled. 'We are a team, doctors and nurses, working together on the same wards,' he said coldly. 'Of course I'm concerned.'

It was a rebuke. She had been unpardonably rude. Now Jon's friendly, affable mood had vanished, to be replaced by a brusque efficiency. Hannah's heart sank into her bedsocks. She'd forgotten her place in the pecking order. Student nurses dared not speak like that to Senior Registrars; she should have been grateful even to have her existence acknowledged! But if Jon Harrington expected her to grovel, then he'd been heading from kick-off for disappointment. Not for Hannah the weeping into the sheets and covering a disdainfully proffered hand with grateful kisses. Oh no! She'd far rather kiss him properly . . . and for very different reasons.

Her cheeks turned pink beneath the bruises. 'I am very grateful to you, Doctor,' she insisted with grave dignity. 'And I do thank you for your concern. If you hadn't arrived on the scene when you did,' she added with a rash affectation of brightness, 'I should now be on a slab in the mortuary instead of taking up one of your precious beds.'

Jon frowned as if Hannah had just made a joke in very bad taste, grimaced with exasperation over his patient's determination to make light of her ordeal. 'How charmingly you put it,' he observed with dry irony, unfolding his great height and flexing his muscles. With a stay of his hand he quelled her murmur of repeated gratitude. 'Now you're to go straight home this afternoon.' I'd take you myself if I wasn't tied up, he thought grimly. 'Make sure that for once you do as I say'.

Heading for the door, he delivered

his parting shot across one arrogant
shoulder.

'And don't come back till your face
bears looking at once more!'

6

'You're a sight for sore eyes, you are, Nurse!' called out one of the porters as Hannah dashed back from the dry-cleaners with her navy jacket, cheeks glowing and hair wind-tossed to a tangle. She paused, gasping for breath, and smiled at Jack in his cosy niche by the main entrance. He was such a nice man — always a cheery word for the staff as they came and went. 'You should have seen me the week before last, Jack,' she told him. 'All black eyes and bruises, I was!'

'Aye,' nodded the porter, sucking on his briar pipe, 'we heard about that. Dr Harrington saved your life then, lassie.'

Hannah's bottom lip furled at the reminder. 'Have to fly — on duty at half-past twelve. Be seeing you, Jack!' She set off at a gallop, luxuriating in the knowledge that nurses in uniform might never run within the hospital grounds — but nurses in jeans could do as they please. She filled her lungs with great gasps of icy air . . . great stuff, even if it had passed through fifty thousand other respiratory systems first. Ah, but it was good to be back.

Hannah tumbled into her room and turned the jacket out of its paper bag. Yes, thank the lord, they had made an invisible job of mending it. Almost as good as new. With Christmas coming up fast, the expense of replacing her only winter coat would have been one big headache.

Food . . . and it had better be snappy. Some of Mother's home-made pâté, stashed safely in Hannah's tiny fridge. Mmm, but it smelled delicious — garlicky chicken liver pâté with some of those cracker biscuits; what a brilliant cook Mum was, when she tore herself away from her looms and threads and dyes.

She made it to Grenville with three minutes to spare.

Dr Harrington came up to the ward during patients' lunches and was closeted with Sister in her office for quite some time. Every time Hannah's eyes swivelled towards that door it was still closed, which meant 'not to be interrupted'. Hannah supposed they must be having a very important review of all the patients, but when she mentioned this to Staff Nurse Phillips it seemed she'd guessed wrong. It was to do with a revolutionary change of practice concerning the drugs round; Dr Harrington himself was going to explain what he intended to the assembled nursing staff. Meantime, he and Sister French were looking at the way ward routine might be affected. Grenville was to take part in an experiment.

'Keep an eye on Mr Benny,' advised Staff Phillips. 'He wants to take himself to the loo, and we must encourage his sense of independence.' The helping hand must be tactful and discreet, and Nurse Westcott could always be relied upon to handle patient-care with sensitivity. 'He's very shaky — even with a zimmer,' murmured Hannah, observing the old man as he shuffled past with his walking frame. 'I can't see how he'll manage to live alone after this last stroke.' It was so sad to think of the poor old chap, struggling on in his little home after his wife's death not six months previously. She saw him safely back to his bed and tucked a blanket lovingly about the skin-and-bone knees. 'Now what about some more of that lime juice you're so fond of?'

'Nurse Westcott! I should like to see you in the office.'

Hannah swung around in sudden and inexplicable agitation. She hadn't seen Jon for over a week. The sound of his voice made her two hands tremble, her insides judder and lurch in sickening upheaval. 'Yes, Doctor . . . ' she managed breathlessly. What was this? Praise? A ticking off? That quizzical regard gave nothing away.

Jon swung on his heel and headed

back to Sister's office, no doubt expecting Hannah to trail subordinately in his wake. She took her time, with deliberation measuring just the right amount of cordial into a glass and adding fresh water from the jug on Mr Benny's locker. 'Are your pillows comfortable now, dear? Anything else you need? How about your glasses and a read of your paper?'

'Just going to sit and watch the world go by, Nursie. Now don't you be keepin' yon doctor waiting. Looks the sort to kick up a storm if 'e doesn't get his own way.'

Hannah forced a reassuring smile in spite of the tension in her spine. 'I'm here to look after *you*, Mr Benny — not to play doctors' handmaiden.'

'Dr Harrington is in the office, Nurse Westcott,' interrupted a firm voice at Hannah's elbow, and turning, she looked up at Sister French, not two steps away from the locker and clearly mulling over her student nurse's defiant assertion.

'Thank you, Sister. I was just making Mr Benny comfortable.'

The senior nurse walked down the ward with Hannah. 'Doctor's time is valuable, Nurse. You can finish your work when he's gone. I take your point that we're not professional handmaidens, and indeed I would defend it. However, you have been injured and Dr Harrington is concerned to check that you're now fit for duty.'

Through the window of the office loomed the ominous person of the Registrar, contemplating Sister and student nurse with a certain impatience. Hannah summoned up a little spurt of indignation to help her face Jon once more. Why was he bothering with this charade? Of course she was fit for work! Even the bit of infection in her lower lip had quite cleared up.

'Dr Harrington has had no lunch yet,' urged Sister, pricking Hannah's conscience. 'Hurry along now!'

Mango had once described the Registrar as the sort of man who'd eat raw steak for breakfast. What was his favourite lunch? wondered Hannah, as she presented herself for inspection. Minced nurse flambé?

'The reluctant heroine,' was Jon Harrington's dry comment as she appeared in the doorway. He indicated that Hannah should close the door behind her and step across to the window to be examined closely in full daylight. It was dreadfully embarrassing, the way he took hold of her head in both hands, tilting it up to his, just like on the films. Hannah didn't know where to look, so compromised by closing her eyes and holding her breath. 'Ve-ry good. Ve-ry ve-ry good. Give it a day or two, then you'll be back in the kissing market again.'

Hannah's eyes snapped wide. 'I beg your pardon?' she said, entirely taken aback.

'Tell your boyfriend to hold off for a bit longer. Unless you want me to tell him for you.' Jonathan was rubbing the back of his neck as if stooping down to examine her had given him a crick.

Hannah was furious. 'Really, Dr Harrington! I don't know what gives you the right to make such assumptions about me and Dr Fuller!' Her shoulders heaved and the pent-up resentment against Jonathan Boyd-Harrington and all his unwarranted interference in her private life came boiling to the surface. 'Frankly, I should be grateful if you would give me credit for being able to handle my own affairs.' Damn, that wasn't the right word to use in this context. 'I wasn't born yesterday, you know. I *can* look after myself, whatever else you may believe.' None of this was making sense to the clearly mystified Registrar, but once the flow had started Hannah plunged wildly on into the rapids. 'I'd like you to know I *hate* sugar and I'm far from *sweet*. And . . . and . . . it's been a good many years since the nuns let me out for a weekend exeat!'

She couldn't remember exactly who had said what as the three doctors lounged in idleness beside that glorious swimming pool. It was sufficient that Jonathan had been an amused participant, joining in with those snide comments about her *innocent* looks. How dared he pretend her outburst was beyond rational comprehension! Trying to control that flicker of a grin as he watched the uptilted angry face of his erstwhile patient ... 'My dear good girl, there must be some mistake — '

'Oh, you made a mistake all right, taking me for an insipid and over-protected little church mouse. For two years I've wanted to tell you that I think you're absolutely despicable!'

'Good God, Hannah,' complained her tormentor, 'what a hell of a whiff of garlic! Which reminds me, *I* haven't eaten yet, if you quite clearly have.' He was using her Christian name as casually as if they were the dearest of friends. 'Here, let me feel your head. I may have overlooked something in my diagnosis ... a fever, perhaps? Brain damage?'

Hannah retreated as far from him as possible till her back was up against the reassuring solidity of the door. From the ward she knew well enough that only the bulk of the doctor would be visible through the glass partition. Framed against the window and the November murk of the city, his massive body blocked out the small natural light. Her heart was hammering within her breast, her breathing laboured and clearly audible. Either Jon Harrington was as great an actor as his friend Marcus Shero, or he truly was at a loss and could not recall what he'd said about her that day in France. She'd better remind him, quick. Wasn't it what she'd been longing to do all the while, ever since that day in Lecture Room 3?

'I was in France with Mango Fitzpatrick. The day you and your brother arrived — and ruined my . . . my friendship with Richard Derby.'

Jon folded his arms and tilted his head back, giving Hannah the benefit of one of his famous slow and heavy-lidded stares. So that was it! Yes, he remembered that visit. 'Well now,' he drawled with all the arrogance of the man of more mature years. She was exaggerating, of course. But still . . . 'Then I did you a good turn, didn't I? From what Sebastian's told me, Dick Derby's broken more hearts than you've had hot dinners.'

Hannah's eyes were wild as a vixen's at bay. She didn't know what possessed her at that moment, but with one lunge she was so close to Jon Harrington she could feel the heat of his body through the thin material of her uniform dress. Then her arm raised and she whipped undone the striped bow-tie, saying as she did so, 'And *you*, Dr Harrington, have broken *mine*!'

★　★　★

The ward kitchen was an oasis of calm. Hannah pulled open the fridge and buried her burning face in its cool interior, making a hopeless pretence of counting the milk bottles for the evening drinks. Gradually her breathing steadied to a controllable rate and the pain in her chest subsided. Heavy footsteps strode past and she heard the mute slam of the swing doors in Jon's wake. He could not have stayed to report her to Sister French, then, who was chatting to patients in the day room.

Perhaps Jon was going straight to the chief nursing officer! Insolence was a heinous offence in the world of hospitals, where lives depended on people working together in peace and harmony and taking instructions and orders from their seniors.

Hannah buried her face in her hands and feverishly scolded herself for having behaved totally unprofessionally. There was nothing for it but to seek out Dr Harrington and subject herself to the utmost humiliation. 'But I'm *not* truly sorry! If I had my chance again, I'd say it all, every word. But I wouldn't untie the . . . oh, hell's bells! What a dreadful thing to have done. I think I feel sick . . . '

Desperate to keep busy, Hannah fled into the ward and sought out Sister. What if they threw her out of the Hanoverian? banned her from the Royal College of Nursing, told every training school in the land to avoid like the plague one Hannah Mary Rachel Westcott? 'You wanted me to do a full history on the patient admitted this morning, Sister. Shall I see to that now?'

Ellen French was puzzled by the naked pleading in Westcott's anxious hazel eyes. Whatever was the matter with the girl? She looked as if she'd been given six months to live, instead of a clean bill of health from Dr Harrington. 'What have you been eating, dear? I'm afraid I can't let you near my patients breathing fumes like that!'

Macbride was listening and her sharp eyes gleamed with pleasure to see Westcott's discomfiture. 'Perhaps if she rinsed her mouth out with Lysol, Sister,' she suggested sweetly, smirking at Hannah behind Ellen French's back.

The Ward Sister pursed her lips; she'd been under the impression these two were getting on better than might have been expected in view of the Senior Tutor's warning. At any rate Macbride was acquitting herself responsibly enough — though her manner with patients tended to be on the abrupt side. Ellen French made a mental note to take the girl on one side and have a quiet word about the way her work was going, with recommendations that Macbride intensify her efforts to implement total patient care.

Westcott, on the other hand, was a born and dedicated nurse. No call to remind *this* one to consider the spiritual and mental well-being of her patients, as well as their more obvious physical needs.

Not that Westcott was perfect.

Sister finished her tour of the ward and went into her office. Now to tackle some of the routine administration and hope for an uninterrupted half hour. Leaning back in her chair, she tapped her front teeth with a pencil. Should she comment on Westcott's attitude to Dr Harrington when making her report? Some nurses, it was true, had a chip on their shoulders where doctors were concerned, seeing them as demigods who expected to be treated likewise by their dutiful handmaidens. This made the nurses react aggressively. And handmaiden was the word young Westcott had used — as if she had just cause to dislike Jonathan Harrington.

'And maybe she has at that,' mused Ellen French. 'How do I know what goes on in their private lives? Still, I've seen J.H. giving that young lady some very perplexed looks, when he didn't suspect he was being observed. Normally I shouldn't take a bit of notice . . . except that Registrars do not as a rule concern themselves with the student nurses on the wards. Yes, this is both puzzling and peculiar. And if it affects Westcott's work on my ward I shall consider it my bounden duty to haul her over the coals.'

★ ★ ★

In the Sisters' sitting room the two nurses in charge of medical wards Braybrooke and Grenville were swapping notes and problems. Sister Junor had slipped off her laced shoes, elevating her splendid lower limbs on the arm of a convenient easy chair, the frilled cap which usually crowned the luxuriant, glossy pleat of her chestnut hair nesting in the lap of her dark blue dress. Ellen French was as usual knitting: her hands were never idle. She not only ran her ward with maximum efficiency, but her home and her three children too.

'Yes,' meditated Junor, looking well pleased with life in general, 'work's turned out a sight more interesting since the arrival of You Know Who. Am I glad they didn't after all appoint that woman from St George's! She wouldn't have been half so impressive.'

With a twitch of her lips Sister French responded dryly that for a woman to have reached *that* level of competence was impressive in itself. Personally she'd have liked to see a woman hold down a senior job in medicine at the Hanoverian.

Grace just closed her eyes and pictured Jon Harrington. Ellen was being deliberately obtuse; she knew very well it wasn't his brain that was fascinating the nursing staff! Oh yes, the grapevine had been buzzing with speculation ever since that compelling addition strode on to the hospital scene. Word had got around that he was playing hard to get: but whatever it was he wanted, Grace was confident she had it in abundance. And she wasn't averse either to making the first move. 'Give you three guesses who I wouldn't mind bumping into under the mistletoe this year!'

Ellen was trying to count stitches. 'The chaplain?' she suggested innocently.

Junor's coarse laugh echoed round the room. 'If you mean that R.C. padre, I always did rise to a challenge!' She reached for her handbag and lit a cigarette, exhaling blue smoke in a stream from her ruby-red lips. Much more flamboyant than her quiet counterpart on Grenville, Grace Junor was still unattached. She was fond of saying there weren't enough *real* men about to grab her interest for long enough to contemplate marriage. She was certainly highly popular with the opposite sex, thanks to her bold personality and striking good looks. 'You know me well enough by now, Sister French. My mind's been on the Harrington track since the day he walked into the Hanoverian. I'll get him by New Year, that I promise you. Oh, by the way, is your second-year back? The one I had on my ward for twenty-four hours' observation. The girl who was nearly raped.'

'She is indeed. In fact . . . '

'Yes?'

But Ellen just shook her head. Idle

conjecture was never her style. Anyway, it was the vaguest feeling, nothing of any substance really. Whatever it was she sensed between the Registrar and her student nurse it was far from being a *romance* — even though it was rumoured Dr Harrington had been instrumental in rescuing Nurse Westcott from being throttled to death. Gratitude, in Sister French's judgment, appeared far from uppermost in that young woman's mind, the way she'd been spotted *glowering* at the Registrar's impervious broad back.

Sister Junor dragged on her cigarette, screwing up her eyes against the smoke. 'I really go for these very tall guys,' she said reflectively. 'Specially if they're well built like dear Jon. I'm a big girl myself — no denying it — but up against that physique it feels like I'm in a rain shadow.' She nudged the other Sister good-humouredly, interrupting the steady rhythm of the knitting needles. 'Oh, go on — you may well smile. I know you think I've got sex on the brain.'

'Indeed I do not,' interrupted Ellen French with calm certainty. 'A fly on the wall might take you for a man-eating spider. But fortunately I've worked here long enough to know you wouldn't be in a position of such responsibility — not at a hospital with our reputation — if you weren't first rate at your job. And I've seen that for myself. Why you haven't married before, though . . . well, only you know the answer to that one.'

Junor purred with satisfaction. 'Mr Right has only just turned up on my horizon. And I'm admitting this to you alone, Ellen, but I find him very, very compelling.'

Ellen laid her knitting on her lap and carefully measured the length from ribbing to armhole. 'Being happily married myself, I fear I seek other qualities in Registrars than animal magnetism.'

'Such as what?'

'We-ell, Jon Harrington is clearly a very clever physician. On ward rounds I'm aware that Sir Freddy accords him a very respectful ear — you'll have noticed that too. Mmm. No doubt has him lined up for the firm's next junior consultant post.'

'So?'

Sister French shrugged her neat navy-blue shoulders and the frills on her cap bobbed with the tilt of her head. 'I find him a bit too ... super cool. Uninvolved.' She sighed thoughtfully. 'Rather intimidating, I must confess. My nice Dr Fuller turns into a bumbling idiot when Harrington appears on the scene. Poor fellow, a houseman's lot is not a happy one.'

A delicious shiver tingled Grace Junor's spine. 'I just *adore* an intimidating man!' Her eyes had gone all dreamy and far-away. 'Jon Harrington's very good with my ladies. Not matey like the last Registrar, but charming all the same. There's a sense of real concern there.'

'Concern for the patient? Or concern to solve the presenting problem — the challenge to his diagnostic skills? As I see it, Harrington's aim is to come up with the right answer: alleviating suffering is not his first priority.'

'You make him sound like a computer, not a physician!' Grace Junor was all indignation. 'I entirely disagree. But that just adds to his fascination, don't you think? Such a complex and provoking personality. All that, attached to a James Bond physique and a face that looks as if the Greek god has been in a fight over some Helen of Troy and got his heart-throb profile ruined. Dangerous-looking man!'

Junor indulged in a delicious shiver of anticipation of the time when she and Jon Harrington would declare their mutual passion . . . Sister French saw it and laughed. 'You must have heard the tale. *Never* dates nurses, only rich society ladies. You'll have to give up the *Nursing Mirror* and take the *Tatler* instead.' She chuckled as an idea began to take seed. 'Keep trying, though, love. The humanising influence of a good woman could be just what the doctor needs.'

Junor's beautifully pencilled eyebrows soared towards her auburn hairline. 'Change that to *bad* woman, please do. I assure you my intentions towards Heartbreaker Harrington are strictly dishonourable. So roll on the mistletoe season! I intend to administer a dose of some ancient and very potent medicine before this year is out . . . now that you and I have diagnosed Dr Harrington's complaint!'

7

Pete was just hilarious — clowning in jeans and a sweater with darned elbows and covered in dust from the rehearsal room floor, even so, he could conjure up the pantomime image of Beauty's elder Ugly Sister. Hannah laughed till her sides ached, totally relaxed and unself-conscious because Jon Harrington was on call and couldn't possibly turn up that night.

'How many rehearsals did I miss when I was off sick?' she whispered to the medical secretary playing the balletic Fairy.

'One with Marcus Shero, two with Dr Kennedy and Dr Harrington.'

'Oh dear — as many as that? It's all taking shape so quickly. Some people already know their lines, word-perfect!' Hannah chewed at her thumbnail, wondering if Jon would recall his threat to give her some personal coaching. After the way she'd lost control of her tongue she wasn't keen to face that tormenting man in a hurry. Her mind simply refused to grapple with the outcome of it all, now that it was clear the dreaded instant dismissal wasn't going to happen. In her heart she knew Jon could be relied upon to devise punishment to match the recklessness of her crime.

Hannah had to imagine herself locked away in the castle of the Beast, while her horrible sisters and beastly brothers lived it up at a local Ball. She was supposed to be off-stage, gazing into her magic mirror and sorrowing for her father, who was reflected back to her on his sickbed, neglected by the rest of his selfish family. Marcus Shero was effortlessly dominating the evening's rehearsal with his charismatic personality and the towering weight of all that theatrical experience.

'Come on, folks, I want a tremendous wattage — a *tremendous* vitality level.

Each one of you — say to yourself, 'Hey, folks, look at *me*!'' As the pace of the evening heated up, he threw off his oxblood leather jacket to reveal a waistline that had been in better shape and was not enhanced by a close-fitting white tee-shirt. Still, to Pete and Hannah the man was just magic. By the end of the rehearsal the whole cast was on a high and departed en masse for the Lamb and Flag. Hannah hung around, fascinated by the proximity of her idol, who was holding a post-mortem with the rest of the production side.

'How's about making me a nightcap over in the Home?' suggested Pete hopefully, but at that moment Marcus signalled to Hannah to join him, and Pete had to stand in the doorway and scowl as he watched his girl being given a hug and a peck on the cheek by the great man himself. 'What was he saying?' nagged Pete jealously when she came back, her cheeks all pink and her face wreathed in smiles. 'And what was it he gave you?'

'Oh . . . nothing,' fibbed Hannah breathlessly, her fingers sliding over the glossy little packet stashed into her jeans' pocket. No good telling Pete — he'd only get even more embarrassingly possessive. 'What a fabulous evening! And you were just terrific, Pete, leaping around like a scalded cat. Those seven brothers are going to make a nice lugubrious comedy team wearing green surgical gowns!'

Back in her room, Hannah transferred that precious little gift to the pocket of the clean uniform she'd hung out ready for the morning — so she could take it out from time to time and remind herself that the treat to come was really not a figment of an over-stimulated imagination.

Seven-thirty on Grenville, though, soon got her feet back on terra firma.

'Dr Harrington admitted a new patient last night,' said Sister French, checking the Kardex record as she briefed her day staff on the state of the ward. 'Robert Gilmore, medical student. Dr Fuller will be doing tests for hepatitis this morning. Now you've been assigned to do a clinical project on hepatitis, Nurse Macbride. I should like you to draw up the care plan for this patient.'

'Me?' responded Marta in pleased surprise at being selected instead of the angelic Westcott. 'I mean — certainly, Sister.' Working on Grenville, she'd now decided, was actually turning out not half bad. Ellen French was fair: and she believed in encouraging rather than nagging. Marta actually smiled, and Hannah noticed that yes, she looked most attractive without that habitual sneer.

'Sam has been moved into the side ward and the chaplain is with him saying the last rites. Please be especially kind and watchful over his friend Mr Beevers; Dr Harrington wishes to be informed of signs of depression. He'll be visiting the ward several times during the day, so please, Nurses, bear that in mind.'

Hannah stuck out her bottom lip.

Not much sleep then for even a Senior Registrar. That should put him in an irritable mood — which didn't augur well for the day. She and Pete had better steer clear of each other or bullets might fly.

Easier said than done, though, for there was Dr Fuller in the 'clean' utility room, where the equipment was kept for laying up the dressing trolleys — Hannah's first task of the morning; helping himself to various bits and pieces required for tests to be done on Robert Gilmore. Hannah noticed the green packs of disposable IM needles were running low, so she added a handful to the plastic box of supplies. 'So. We have a medical student in one of the side wards. Query hepatitis — '

'And carrying on as if he'd got AIDS,' grumbled Pete. 'Talk about a little knowledge being a dangerous thing! Haven't I got enough on my plate without getting landed with a hypochondriac medical student?'

Hannah was trying to think as she

worked, pulling sterile dressing packs from shelves and loading up the trolleys, listing in her mind the relevant facts ... there were two sorts of hepatitis, labelled A and B. You could pick up A, the infective variety, from swimming in polluted water. A was less serious than B, the serum or blood-borne hepatitis. Liver function tests would have been ordered by Dr Harrington to determine what was wrong with Robert Gilmore.

'Shall you need to do a liver biopsy, then?' she asked.

'Unlikely. I got him to check back over his clinical work for the past few months, and the guy now reckons yes, he can just *faintly* recall pricking himself with a needle, accidentally, when taking blood.' Pete's words were tinged with sarcasm.

'Ah, good. Then it's likely to cut down on the tests if you've got him to remember such an important detail. Dr Beast will give you a pat on the back for that.' Hannah closed the cupboard and swung round to put a gallipot on her trolley. Her jaw dropped foolishly.

'Boot up the backside, you mean. All *I* ever get from your Dr Beast. He wastes none of his bedside charm on me.'

'Dr Fuller!' muttered Hannah with wide-eyed urgency. 'I — er — I think you're wanted.'

There he stood, filling the doorway with his height and his bulk, and inevitably his anger. Stethoscope dangling about his chest, bleep in his top pocket, scarlet bow tie reflecting the bullish light in his eyes. Glowering at the discovery of that lippy young nurse and his idiot houseman wasting the hospital's time in cheap jibes at their elders and betters. Organisation Man, they called him; and now, Dr Beast!

All this was racing through Hannah's mind as she tried to picture the scene through Jon Harrington's eyes. And yes, Jon's deep quiet voice sounded coolly unamused. 'Can you spare me a moment, Doctor?' He didn't even look at Hannah: she might have been invisible.

'In the office, please . . . *Doctor!*'

Pete snapped smartly to attention. 'Yessir.' Jon went ahead and Pete turned back to Hannah, rolling his eyes and making a slicing gesture across his jugular.

For five whole seconds Hannah stood there alone, fingers pressed against her forehead, feeling sick and ashamed. Poor Pete wouldn't be given the chance to say a word in his own defence; Jon would not look beyond the evidence of his ears and eyes: the fact that nurse and doctor had been discussing a patient would be swept aside by the presumptuous Dr Harrington. And you couldn't exactly blame him for feeling outraged.

And worse than that, mourned Hannah, I didn't even mean it. Yes, it was me who nicknamed Jon Dr Beast; but that was when I'd just discovered who he was. I like him now — I really do. But I feel as if I'm on a seesaw where that man is concerned. Permanently on tenterhooks because of the extraordinary way I feel about him. I just can't let it affect my work.

And I can't let Pete suffer because I'm in a tizz over Jon Harrington . . .

Hannah's mind was made up. With bold if suicidal steps she found herself facing the implacable wood of the closed door to the doctors' room, knocked, and was across the threshold before either man could say Jack Robinson.

The doctors, as she had anticipated, were entirely alone. They turned at her entry with expressions of mild enquiry. Hannah stood her ground grimly. Would she be in time to save Pete from being dismissed from Sir Freddy's firm?

No atmosphere of tension. Not even the trace of a blackened eye. Pete's arms were lightly folded, and the Registrar was half-sitting on the desk as he considered the medication sheet held in his right hand, his left gripping not so much his houseman's neck but the edge of the sturdy wooden desk supporting his considerable weight.

'Yes, Nurse?' he enquired brusquely.

Horrified at her mistake, Hannah grasped the first excuse her flailing brain came up with. 'Um . . . ' It was unforgivable, bursting in on the doctors like this. 'Would you like one of Sister's chocolate biscuits, Dr Harrington?'

Jon raised his eyebrows in exaggerated surprise. 'Thank you for thinking of it, Nurse.' He spoke slowly and deliberately as if dealing with an imbecile. 'But not at this moment. Not at . . . ' he was glancing at the gold watch strapped to a solidly sinewy wrist, ' . . . nine-fifteen in the morning.' His eyebrow quirked in amusement and to her horror Hannah saw clearly for the first time what was working its way through the Registrar's thought processes. Here we go. Another of the little darlings with a crush on me. Popping up all over the place to gawp at her beloved.

How galling! Especially, if the truth

could be told — and, dammit, it couldn't now she saw with her own eyes that Pete was perfectly okay — she'd dashed in like St George to save Pete from the fiery breath of Dr Beast's wrath.

Even Pete had cottoned on to the drift of Dr Harrington's thoughts, grinning and winking at Hannah from his safe position to the rear of his boss's broad shoulder.

As she was about to slam the door behind her, Jon's voice summoned Hannah back. 'One moment, Nurse.'

Deliberately Hannah stared past Jon and out of the window, so he should be aware that the sight of his face was perfectly resistible in *her* particular case.

'You and I have to get together some time soon for a private rehearsal — to make up for the ones you missed last week.'

Pete pulled an incredulous face. Hannah stiffened and her mouth went dry.

'Fortunately I can manage this Friday night.'

'Well, I'm afraid I can't!' she declared, triumphantly. 'I'm dining with Marcus Shero on Friday night.'

The effect on Jon Harrington was nothing short of electric. His eyes were like lasers, his voice boomed like a thunderclap. 'What the devil for?'

Pete ranged up behind his Registrar. 'Yes, Hannah! What game d'you think you're playing? You're supposed to have a date with *me*.'

Their combined astonishment and disbelief was most unflattering. It stopped Hannah in her tracks. Was she hallucinating? In the cold light of day an invitation for a student nurse to dine with a theatrical Star with a capital S ... well, it did seem mighty improbable. Jon was glowering as if the temerity was all hers, and her shocking statement the figment of a deranged Shero-worshipper's frantic imagination.

Then on a sharp little indrawn breath she remembered the precious object in her uniform pocket, pressed into her hand by the actor himself when he had whispered that special invitation in her astonished ear. 'Meet me here,' he had said, 'on Friday night, at eight.'

Her hand closed over the little oblong packet and she held it out with defiant dignity. 'There you are. That's where Marcus Shero is taking me!'

It was a glossy yellow packet of matches bearing the name and address of Langan's Brasserie in Piccadilly.

Pete looked at Dr Harrington, and Dr Harrington looked thoughtful. He also looked at Hannah. With her hair drawn back off her face, emphasising the stubborn set of her jaw and the full and pouting mouth, she seemed like a hurt and accusing angel, challenging them to disbelieve her now.

Then, like an angel, she saw her moment and vanished from the doctors' sight.

★ ★ ★

'You're behaving like some stagestruck ingénue!'

Pete was driving recklessly, his old banger surging up St James' with all the abandon of a warhorse that has thrown its knight in shining armour. Hannah felt sick, but she was nervous anyway, so perhaps that wasn't entirely Pete's fault.

'I bet Shero's kicking himself. I bet he woke up next morning and groaned his head off when he remembered what he'd let himself in for.'

'Very probably.'

'What will you do when he starts the seduction bit? Give him a sample of your famous self-defence?'

Hannah managed a weak grin. 'Cheer up, Pete. We're meeting to discuss my rôle in the panto, remember?'

The Citroën shuddered to a halt at their destination. Pete jumped out to open Hannah's door. 'Do I look all right?' she asked anxiously.

'Too right you do. I'll be back for you at eleven.'

They argued fiercely for the next thirty seconds.

I'm not going to be collected like a schoolgirl from a party! fumed Hannah as she watched a scowling Pete drive away. He'd never acted this way before — so jealous and possessive . . . Crossing her fingers that he wouldn't turn up as threatened, she hauled her courage by the bootstrings and made her entrance into one of the most famous restaurants in London.

The first face she clapped eyes upon was very well known indeed.

Jon Harrington! What on earth could he be doing at Langan's, on the very night that she was dining à deux with . . . and there with him at the bar *was* Marcus.

Hannah's assumed sophistication took a nosedive. Worse still, though the two men had seen her hovering uncertainly as the animated throng milled past to deposit their coats and get to the bar, they were just staring, blankly.

It was Marcus who suddenly blinked,

beamed in recognition and raised his glass in greeting. Beside him, Dr Harrington looked simply stunned.

Mango had loaned the slinky Jasper Conran dress and fixed the sophisticated make-up. 'But me no buts,' she had ordered, quelling Hannah's half-hearted protests. 'Dining with Marcus Shero where all the glitterati hang out calls for something *special*!'

And when she'd viewed her friend's handiwork, Hannah had been astonished that she could look quite so soignée. Hair coiled in a soft bun on the nape of her neck, with teased-out tendrils framing her oval face; eyes hugely glowing with silvery shadow, her full mouth a glossy rose-red contrasting with the electric-blue pure silk-satin.

Now, seeing Jon Harrington's shocked expression, Hannah wasn't sure the effect was *quite* so hot.

Next moment the apparent sophistication vanished as Hannah's blankly beautiful face split into a wide smile of relief. Marcus had materialised at her elbow and that voice that thrilled women the world over was proclaiming for all to hear that this young uncertain creature was his guest.

'Darling, you look absolutely ravishing! I *knew* we'd picked the right girl for the part.' Next moment Hannah felt those celebrated hands upon her shoulders as Marcus kissed her, left cheek and then right, his hands sliding down her back to her waist, in no hurry to loose his prize.

Jonathan glowered. Clearly he took a dim view of Hannah in her borrowed fine feathers, the deeply curving neckline and the cling of rich, slippery silk-satin.

In that mood his presence threatened to put a damper on the most exciting night of her whole life, he and Pete between the two of them! Hannah's stubborn bottom lip thrust out in defiance as she saw how Dr Harrington was drumming his fingers on the bar top in a tattoo of irritation. Did he think he was some sort of spy, then?

But for a while Hannah found her attention drawn away from Dr Beast as, wide-eyed, she absorbed her surroundings. Celebrities streamed in, reduced to human proportions, greeting each other noisily and appearing to wander from table to table to see who was dining tonight.

'Now, you lovely creature, what can I get you to drink?'

A half of ginger-beer shandy clearly wasn't in order at Langan's. Not when you were pulling all the stops out to act cool and elegant.

Seeing her hesitate, Marcus suggested an exotic cocktail, and Hannah nodded gratefully, one nervous hand playing with a pearl drop ear-ring as he turned away to the bar and was immediately hailed by George Melly. Abandoning her for interminable seconds of Dr Beast's glowering silence.

. . . Until I let slip about seeing Marcus, Jon knew nothing of it! recalled Hannah. So what *is* he doing here, all tight-lipped and disapproving?

Surely he doesn't share Pete's ridiculous suspicions about Marcus planning to try out his ladykiller technique later? On a nurse from the Hanoverian? A man who has the pick of the world's most beautiful women? I should be so lucky!

The doctor stared down at Hannah's expressive face which was reflecting her fascination with everyone and everything. He felt he should not intrude upon her absorption. Let the girl enjoy herself while she could. He had his own plans for the outcome of this extraordinary evening. But he glanced at his watch with increasing irritation . . . Where the hell was she?

Hannah could think of nothing to say that would interest this man. Accidentally her tight satiny sleeve brushed against his arm and she jumped as if live current ran through her. She already knew enough about Jon Harrington to know he never wasted words — the strong and silent type. Personally, Hannah found Jon far more intimidating than his celebrated friend. Even here, his presence was impossible to ignore. Remote and exclusive, he towered over almost every other man in the place, his formal grey pinstripe relieved by a fuchsia bow-tie, matching silk handkerchief protruding just the right amount from the breast pocket.

His chin, Hannah noted, peeping up at Jon to see where the direction of his gaze lay, was faintly blue-shadowed, as if this particular evening he hadn't had time to shave. It lent an air of ruthlessness that bothered her and made her clear her throat nervously as Marcus returned, bearing a glass of something pink and tasting deliciously of raspberries, as quaffable as lemonade. But not so innocuous. Jon looked at her knocking it back and muttered, 'Steady on!' Hannah glared back in defiance.

Marcus in his dinner suit of royal-blue and black damask was something of a peacock. Not a tall man, he was stocky and barrel-chested, with swarthy good looks and, of course, that seductive rich voice accompanying a supremely confident manner. He was rich and famous, and he revelled in it, coming as he had from a poor background in the North. Hannah found him oddly endearing. A nice man, in spite of the theatricality, shrewd and warm.

'Sup up,' encouraged Marcus. 'Good lass. Another of those, eh?'

'One will be quite sufficient,' put in Jon smoothly. But before the young nurse could voice an indignant protest, he added with evident relief, 'Aha! Camilla, at last.'

Camilla! Hannah's senses quickened with mingled interest and alarm. So Jon did not intend to play gooseberry after all. Curiosity consumed her about this goddess who had captured the divine Dr Harrington. Hannah turned to watch.

She saw Jon's hands first, moving and lifting and reaching out to clasp another woman to his side, heard his voice murmur in intimate greeting, 'Darling, you should have let me pick you up at the Square.'

A very public display of affection, brooded Hannah, proving Dr Beast was flesh and blood after all. And a relationship of some long standing . . .

She raised her eyes, with a strange slow reluctance to come face to face with Jon's kind of woman. And of course Camilla *was* almost improbably lovely. 'But I've seen you before!' gasped Hannah, realising she was staring goggle-eyed at the most sought-after model on the fashion scene. Though Hannah didn't go in for buying glossy magazines, you'd have to be a hermit not to recognise the face that graced covers of *Harper's* and *Vogue*. No wonder Jon wasn't interested *that way* in nurses — especially ones with the added handicap of having been labelled church-mouse vicarage girls.

Hannah was watching Jon and Camilla. Marcus was watching Hannah, shrewdly noting surprise give way to alarm and despondency in those gentle hazel eyes. Sensing that she'd like to run away and hide, he took her firmly by the arm and drew her forward. 'Camilla — meet my young friend Hannah Westcott. Hannah's a student nurse at Jon's hospital.'

He seemed to place special emphasis on those last two words. Making it sound as if Jon owned the place!

'Hi there,' said the vision in a friendly puff of a voice that could only be described as transatlantic Cockney. 'Pleased to meet you, Hannah. Say, but that dress is real pretty. You look super.'

With casual disdain Camilla let her opossum-lined raincoat slither to the floor, trailing it behind her with one finger as she made for a table in the prime spot earmarked for very famous people. Jon grabbed the coat and disposed of it, then joined them as they seated themselves at table. 'I'm absolutely starving,' exclaimed Camilla. 'I could eat a horse!'

She reached up her incredibly slender

arms to loosen and rumple the glossy waterfall of amber hair. That perfect face smiling confidently round Langan's, waving to people she knew, curling delicate white fingers round the stem of her glass of aperitif.

So this is Jon's fiancée, brooded Hannah in awed silence, feeling clumsy and gauche by comparison. Well, the physical match makes sense. She's taller even than Mango! And talk about thin. But she's not a bit snooty. It was nice of her to say she liked my dress.

Camilla was indeed superbly tall and immensely slender. Understatedly chic in a narrow body-skimming tube of fine grey wool jersey against which the mass of her tawny hair glowed. One shoulder was quite bare, and the couturier had sliced away part of the midriff so that when Camilla turned, everyone could see the lower half of her sinuously elegant back. It was all terribly clever and expensive and subtle and sexy. Just as one might expect of an international fashion princess.

'Your face is cold, Millie darling,' murmured Jonathan, his lips brushing the perfection of hollowed cheek. He regarded his prize with fond affection as she laughed at some ribald joke of Marcus's, clinging to Jon's shoulder for support, bronzed fingernails and glossy lips gleaming under the lights. A gilded goddess, reflected Hannah, ever more conscious of her own insignificance. Red lipstick — it was oh, so obvious and old-hat. Blue dresses were for schoolgirls. Or church mice.

'After a month in the States . . . mmm, it's kinda good to be back, you know? I walked here tonight — didn't take a taxi. You can't do *that* on the streets of New York.'

Wow! breathed Hannah silently. I could tell you a tale or two . . . she looked sharply at Jon to see if he would pass any comment, but he was mentioning to Marcus something about needing to get back to the Hanoverian before midnight to do a late round.

Soon they were dipping spoons into

the golden perfection of spinach souffles in individual porcelain dishes. 'I'm famished!' repeated Camilla, rather endearingly for one who looked as if she dined regularly on lettuce leaves. 'I've been with Patrick all afternoon doing a Spring spread for Harper's.' She spooned more anchovy sauce over her souffle and exclaimed in ecstasy.

Dustin Hoffman nodded at Marcus from two tables down and Marcus remembered he wanted a word, leaving Hannah alone with Jon and Camilla to finish her first course.

'I always like long tight sleeves,' said Camilla kindly, noting that Hannah was rather quiet and that her pupils were huge with awe. 'Yours look kinda medieval.'

Hannah smoothed the delicate fabric over her wrists. 'Useful too,' she admitted with a suspicion of a smile, 'they hide my chapped hands.'

Jon and Marcus were now deep in discussion of the pantomime.

'Lanolin rubbed in with sugar works

miracles,' volunteered Camilla, reaching across and feeling the back of Hannah's rough little paws. 'My word, they are sore, you poor kid. You know something? I really admire all you nurses.'

You could almost dislike her for being so darned *nice*, mused Hannah, her empty plate already swept away and replaced by the turbot Marcus had recommended. Camilla was everything a man like Jon Boyd-Harrington could want: glamorous, wealthy, and apparently quite unspoiled by her jet-setting lifestyle. And clearly she was much in love with the highly eligible doctor who dared to call her 'Millie' and tease her with surprisingly gentle banter. They were indeed the perfect couple, though why that was affecting her appetite all of a sudden, and making her heart ache, Hannah truthfully dared not consider.

The panto took over the general conversation and soon Marcus was telling Camilla how Hannah was to play the part of Beauty, with this rare combination of talent and looks that had captivated him at the audition.

Hannah was fearfully embarrassed. 'It's very boring for Camilla if we talk about *Beauty and the Beast*,' she murmured, wriggling in her seat with discomfort at being made the focus of attention. She'd have liked more of that delicious white wine, but for some reason her glass wasn't being filled as frequently as the others'. Then she realised why, catching the almost imperceptible shake of Jon's head as the waiter moved in her direction.

'Thank you,' said Hannah, giving the man a beaming smile that he could not refuse. She lifted her glass and across the rim of it flashed a challenge at Jonathan which clearly warned the doctor that outside the hospital environs she would do as she pleased. Her eyes sparkled, her cheeks glowed with a most becoming warmth, and the heady wine relaxed and stimulated at one and the same time.

Far from being bored with their discussions, Camilla joined in with ideas and suggestions of her own. Bright as well as beautiful, decided Hannah, wondering if her eyes were especially green tonight with wishing she'd been blessed with a few of Jon's fiancée's attributes. She drained her glass again, this time a rich red wine, and realised she'd been staring at Dr Harrington for the last five minutes with dangerously unguarded admiration. Camilla was the luckiest woman in the whole wide world. And Jon the most attractive man . . .

'Ever thought of doing some modelling yourself?' asked Camilla. 'You're not really tall enough, but you've a lovely neck and shoulders and you wear clothes very well. Here,' she delved in her black patent clutch bag and produced a card which she passed to Hannah. 'Take the address of my agency, they're always on the look-out for new young faces.'

For the first time that evening Jon spoke to his beloved in less than gentle tones. 'Don't be ridiculous, Millie, putting ideas like that in the girl's head!' He snatched the card out of Hannah's nerveless fingers and handed it back to Camilla. 'She's a nurse, and a good one too. What she looks like is of no consequence at the Royal Hanoverian.'

Interfering again! Hannah's eyes turned fiery. 'Thank you very much, Camilla. I appreciate the thought, and I'll be glad to have that address if I may.' Hannah snatched the card back and slipped it into her shoe. What Jon had said was perfectly true, a nurse's looks were immaterial. All the same, it hurt that he should put her down so, cruelly emphasising the difference between her and his lovely fiancée. Camilla's hands were so encrusted with rings it was difficult to say whether or not the two were engaged — but more than likely, guessed Hannah miserably. If only she could find a man just like Jon Harrington and just for herself. So he was far from perfect — arrogant and domineering and with standards of perfection that would tax the patience of a saint. But as a doctor he was among the finest and most dedicated, and as a man he was mysterious and masterful and the fulfilment of any woman's dreams . . .

Marcus was being so attentive this evening, treating Hannah as though she were fascinating and desirable — to some men at least. Touching her hand, her arm, her shoulder. Gazing into her eyes, flattering her with praise of her singing and playing of the piano. And he had some absolutely terrific ideas for the panto. 'Who wants a bally fairy queen?' he roared, thumping the table and attracting the attention of other diners. 'You must have got a plastic surgeon tucked away in that hospital of yours, Jon. Bring him on with a scalpel to do a quick face job on the Beast and transform him into your charming prince who captivates Beauty. It'll raise a lot more laughs than some poor idiot in a puffy skirt tottering on her pointes and flagging away with a bit of tinsel on a stick.' He hugged Hannah, who spilled a raspberry on the tablecloth and got cream all down her chin . . . but was sufficiently mellow to care about neither.

'I say, is that the time?' Camilla exclaimed. 'I have to be up at five-thirty.'

'And I've a late round to do tonight,' said Jon firmly, looking at his watch. 'If you'll see Camilla safely home, I'll get this young lady back to her quarters.'

So taken aback was Hannah that she couldn't think up a reasonable protest. And neither Camilla nor Marcus seemed to be about to argue, since Jon's suggestion was, under the circumstances, perfectly sensible and practical since he and Hannah both were heading for the Royal Hanoverian.

Blow it! glowered Hannah, wishing the evening could have gone on for ever, and fuming because it was Dr Harrington who was determined to break things up when they were all having such a marvellous time. He hasn't seen Camilla for over a month. But he's so determined to keep me under surveillance he's letting Marcus take her home. The man is definitely not human. I doubt if he even has a heart . . . in fact all the evidence is to the contrary. Poor Camilla, I bet she's disappointed he's so unromantic!

If Camilla *was* at all put out she was concealing the fact admirably, disappearing off into the night with Marcus and actually kissing Hannah good night as well as darling Jon. As they walked to the doctor's car, Hannah for the first time realised she'd had quite a lot to drink. There was a ringing in her ears and a woolly sensation in her head which intensified as the chill of the December night stroked her burning skin. But the sensation was far from unpleasant. She felt bold and uncaring and ready to say whatsoever she pleased.

And with Jon at the wheel, miles away from the confines of the Hanoverian, here for the first time ever was her chance, her perfect opportunity to tell him exactly how she felt. She waited till he turned the key in the ignition, then launched the first of her heart-seeking missiles . . .

8

Jon, however, fired his salvo first.

'Give me that card of Camilla's!' he demanded curtly, settling himself behind the wheel and waiting while Hannah fumbled with her seatbelt — fingers usually so deft and certain with delicate nursing procedures rendered clumsy by too many glasses of unaccustomed, heady wine.

Her breath caught on a gasp of indignation; Jon Harrington certainly knew how to throw his weight around! She decided on the instant that silence was the safest tactic, staring mutely out of the side window as the Christmas lights winked and sparkled in the frosty night above Regent Street's wide thoroughfare.

Jon cursed in irritation as a car packed with sightseers gawping at the lights drifted aimlessly across the traffic lanes. 'Those kids ought to be in their beds!'

Hey ho, sighed Hannah to herself, obstinately refraining from comment. Season of goodwill, and all that. Of course, you yourself won't let up for an instant, will you, Doctor? You'll be there on duty, from choice, right through the festive season . . . and I'm working over Christmas too. I wonder if I dare give you a peck on the cheek under the mistletoe . . . perhaps like in the fairy story, you might change from Dr Beast into a gorgeous prince come to sweep me away on your dashing white steed.

She settled back into the squishy leather seat and thought that this car wasn't a bad substitute for a dashing white steed. And in a way, Jon Harrington was stealing her off into the night! If only dreams could come true . . . I'd put up a token struggle, imagined Hannah; just for show. But oh, what it would be like to find yourself entrapped in those powerful arms and held close against that pounding heart . . .

What a joke! Where was the evidence that Jon ever had a heart? He seemed bereft of normal feelings; and the way he'd treated Camilla tonight was further proof that he lived only for medicine.

Jonathan's voice broke the silence. He was still fulminating over that wretched model agency's card, and Hannah came back to reality with a shiver. It was still there in her shoe, shiny and sharp-edged against her instep.

'It's a perfectly ridiculous proposition. Camilla ought to know better, raising your hopes like that.'

'Please don't concern yourself on my account,' insisted Hannah huffily. The irony of it! After practically ruining her life once upon a time, here was Jon Harrington demonstrating concern for her moral welfare; sacrificing a passionate reunion with his beautiful girlfriend, just to steer one insignificant little Hanoverian nurse out of the clutches of Marcus Shero — his most generous and helpful friend. With pals like Harrington, muttered an ironic little voice inside Hannah's woozy head, who needs enemies? And if Jon did but know it, she was quite capable of saying no, perfectly nicely, to the charismatic Shero. If indeed — and this Hannah most sincerely doubted — his intentions were other than strictly honourable.

'When I was five,' she remembered dreamily, 'if anyone fell over in the school playground I used to pick them up and comfort them and help my teacher with the iodine and sticking plasters. Nursing — nursing is in my blood, Dr Harrington. I'd never find happiness doing any other kind of work, however glamorous.'

'Good,' said Jon, apparently unmoved by such tender revelations. 'Then you will not object to handing over that card.'

Hannah swivelled her head against the head-rest until his profile was in view, the purple-grey eyes fixed on the road ahead and that thick lock of dark hair spilling across the right side of his forehead. She winced as the slight movement emphasised the ringing sensation within her skull, the heaviness of her eyelids. The sophisticated hairdo was beginning to cascade into dishevelment, but who cared, now all the fun was over and Jon was cross with her. She had seen, with her own astounded eyes, the breathtaking reality of Camilla. What hope then of impressing a man like Jonathan Harrington?

Ah well, yawned Hannah, might as well be hanged for a sheep as a lamb. She wriggled sensuously against the smooth, cool upholstery, letting her coat slip from her shoulders. 'What do you think of my dress, Jon?' She stuck out her chest to show off a plunging neckline that would be wasted on the pin-thin Camilla. The light of mischief stole into greeny-hazel eyes. 'I borrowed it from Nurse Fitzpatrick. You remember Mango, don't you? She fixed my face, too.'

For a leisurely second her chauffeur

took his eyes from the road. The tone of his voice was devastating in its lack of enthusiasm. 'I prefer that outfit you wore for your audition.'

Well, blow me! Hannah grimaced in disgust. What a put-down. My sister's cast-offs are considered more suitable than Mango's expensive and sexy gown!

'Most of all, I like to see you in your uniform,' announced Jon surprisingly. Which was a backhanded sort of compliment when you considered hundreds of other nurses wore it too. 'And,' continued the relentless voice of her tormentor, 'as for all that muck on your face, I might have known Mango Fitzpatrick would have had a hand in it. That young woman, Hannah, is a bad influence on you.'

At this Nurse Westcott sat bolt upright, tugging at the confines of her seatbelt, accusing eyes firing Exocets at the imperturbable doctor, who was braking smoothly as the traffic lights ahead glowed amber. 'I bet you knew who we were right from the start.'

Jon grinned, revealing a regular set of white teeth that gleamed in the shadowy interior of the Jaguar. 'You were kind enough recently to jog my memory concerning some of the finer details of our encounter. Putting two and two together, I'd suggest someone must have been listening in on a private conversation. And . . . '

His hand reached down from the steering wheel so swiftly that Hannah flinched, only to blush in secret as she realised his intention was simply to change gear and not to slap her on the wrist for misbehaviour.

' . . . you know what they say about eavesdroppers. Not that anyone was blackening your character, as I recall. Quite the opposite.'

'You told Dickie I was an unsuitable girlfriend!'

Jon wrinkled his broad brow.

'Totally unsuitable,' repeated Hannah hotly. 'What business was it of yours? You knew nothing whatsoever about me. After you and Sebastian had left,

Dickie was like a stranger. I haven't seen him since that holiday in France. You broke my heart, you beast!' Deep down she was aghast to hear the shrill pitch of her own voice: but the words were out. They could not be bitten back.

There was a moment of silence during which she fought against a sensation of sheer panic. Then Jon responded in that irritatingly cool and rational manner that always had the effect of making her realise that once more she'd only succeeded in making a fool of herself.

'My dear girl! Such a talent for exaggeration. You know, there are occasions, Hannah, when I find you the most aggravating creature. Let me tell you that in Sister's office you came mighty close to getting your bottom smacked.'

Hannah turned crimson and shielded her face with a defensive hand. If her company was so unpleasant, why was Jon driving as if part of a funeral cortege? At this rate, they'd be lucky to see the Royal Hanoverian before breakfast!

Her heart was beating like a tom-tom, even though she'd been relieved of her burden of resentment now that it was all out in the open between them. For his part, Jon appeared totally oblivious of the effect he was having upon his young companion, continuing in that sardonic manner, 'You silly girl. Surely you realise by now it was a master stroke, my extracting you from that tangle with Derby? When I told him you were unsuitable, I meant it. And my tactic clearly worked, since you've transferred your affections to Pete Fuller. Not that he's much of an improvement!'

Nails digging into the palms of her hands, Hannah said tightly, 'Dr Fuller is no more than a very good friend. I wish you wouldn't keep harping on the subject of my so-called 'affairs'. What kind of a girl do you take me for? And what must I do to convince you that

I'm not involved with anyone these days? It took me a long time to get over Dickie. I was genuinely . . . in love. It was you who so heartlessly killed that relationship for me.' The break in her voice owed more to the rising sense of hysteria at being confined in close proximity with a man who cared not one fig for the turbulent sensations he aroused in vulnerable student nurses.

At last Jon seemed to grasp the fact that Hannah was genuinely upset. The warmth of his hand closed over the tense fingers twisting in her lap. 'Poor little Hannah!' His amusement was so hurtfully evident that Hannah snatched her hand away — regretting the impulse even as she did so. Punishing her own foolish, prickly self.

'I want you to know,' she gasped, breathing deep and hard as if she'd just run a marathon, 'that I was deeply hurt by Dick Derby. For some months I could scarcely eat. My friends were convinced I was anorexic!'

'Anorexic . . . or should it be

anorectic?' wondered Jon, apparently more concerned over the niceties of grammar than Hannah's physical decline and his own culpability. He gave her a brief sidelong appraisal as the traffic lights illuminated her pale face with a greenish tinge. 'You seem pretty healthy-looking nowadays — though I did consider you a mite undernourished when we were doing that physiology demo. In fact tonight I've admired you in quite a different light: grown up at last into a beautiful, desirable woman.'

From the depths of misery Hannah soared now to the heights. Beautiful? Who, me? . . . She bit her lip, suspecting more of Jon's merciless brand of teasing.

Only picture Camilla. Think of Marcus Shero. For what unfathomable reason could Jon be exercising his mesmeric charm?

Don't lose your head, warned Hannah's sane and sensible core. Keep your two feet stuck to the ground. And, inexorably as a punctured balloon, her mood deflated. But her trembling fingers yearned to feel once more the comforting warmth of Jon's hand clasping hers in the secret darkness.

Why had he come to Langan's tonight? Because clearly he had, like Pete, considered her unable to cope with a man as worldly and sophisticated as Shero; and having introduced the two of them, he felt responsible. But beautiful, he'd said . . . and how could a girl hang on to her common sense, trapped in a sleek limousine with a fascinating doctor who murmured words like that into her eager ear?

Hannah sighed theatrically and fluttered her enviable lashes with a sidelong glance at Jon, whose sleeve was brushing against her bare arm. 'I truly believed I was in love with Dickie Derby,' she murmured wistfully, as if musing aloud, oblivious of Jon's heady presence.

'Of course you did,' he responded heartily. 'We've all been 'in love' in our time. We get over it.' Cheerfully unsympathetic was the only way to describe his manner, and Hannah felt not a little sorry for herself. Wasn't that just typical? Love. A disease to be treated most successfully by neglect. Ignore the symptoms and they'll go away. One of those psychosomatic upsets of the nervous system.

That poor girl Camilla. How had the two of them ever got involved in the first place? It wasn't strictly Jon's own fault, of course, since his emotional development must have been severely stunted by the trauma of his parents' marriage. Cold, and hard, and unfeeling in his personal relationships. Hannah frowned in painful concentration as a thought speared into her befuddled brain.

'You know what I think?' she blurted out of the blue.

Jon raised his eyelids the merest fraction.

'I think you're the most unromantic man in the world.'

Was he grinning? . . . He was!

'You've let Camilla go home with your best friend,' she pursued.

He was nodding agreement. That could not be denied.

'And all because for some peculiar reason you see yourself as the guardian of the Hanoverian nurses' morals. Are you afraid of sex, Dr Harrington? Is that your problem?'

As soon as it came out, Hannah could have bitten off her foolish, reckless tongue. For Jon was leaving the main roads for a murky side street, gliding into the kerb and well out of the range of the nearest street light.

Inside the limousine it was a warm, dark cave, silent but for the gasp of Hannah's ragged breathing as the doctor leaned towards her, one arm resting across the back of her seat, the other . . .

'Don't touch me!' shrilled Hannah, like an escapee from a convent. But the hand had passed her and was delving into the glove compartment for a bunch of keys. Damn! Damn! Damn! Disappointment far outweighed relief. She sat there feeling about six inches high.

'Now who's afraid?' observed Jon Harrington blandly, in no great haste to remove his dark bulk as he trapped her defenceless form. He was laughing at her! teasing his victim, jingling his keys in front of her nose, his face so close she could feel the stroke of his breath upon her skin. 'My flat is right here. Shan't be five minutes, but I'll lock you into the car to make sure you're safe.'

Make sure I don't escape, grimaced Hannah; but her tongue had got her into quite enough trouble for one night, so she kept her reservations to herself. True to his word Jon was soon back, carrying a black medical bag which he laid upon the back seat with far more care than he treated his women. Seeing that in his absence his passenger had buttoned her coat up tight to her throat, Jon captured Hannah's wary eye and gave her a knowing wink. A frivolous gesture, and singularly disconcerting, coming as it did from the humourless Dr Beast.

He parked in the doctors' car park and insisted on seeing his charge right to the door of the Nurses' Home

— where he kissed her cheek in perfunctory fashion and patted her on the bottom before sending her in with instructions to get straight to her bed. On a miraculous surge of adrenalin Hannah came wide awake, racing up the stairs two at a time, one hand clasping reverently the cheek Jon's lips had brushed, in an ecstasy of happiness.

Even though she'd behaved so badly, it hadn't ruined everything. Jon must still quite like her: at any rate he found her amusing as well as aggravating. He'd told her she looked beautiful; and he'd kissed her, albeit unemotionally. Hannah slammed her door and fell back against it, panting. 'I can't wait for the morning!' she informed the silence. 'Can't wait to see Jon again. He really and truly is my hero!'

* * *

Hurrying across to the Wymark building, Hannah met up with Marta and was surprised to notice mascara and pink lipstick — and an alert expression on Macbride's usually sulky face. She looked like somebody in love. 'How's your medical student getting on?' enquired Hannah interestedly. 'I thought the jaundice was less pronounced yesterday when I looked in on him. Underneath all the yellow Robert's a nice-looking chap.'

'They did the Australian antigen test, and Dr Harrington says Rob's picked up a mild serum hepatitis. Easily diagnosed, he says, but unfortunately there isn't a specific treatment. Just a light fat-free diet till Rob begins to get his appetite back. Bed-rest for a couple of weeks, then he's going home to convalesce — oh, and strictly no alcohol until the tests prove normal again.'

'Poor chap. I suppose this illness will mess up his medical studies. Still, he's lapping up all your TLC, Marta. When I popped my head round the door, his face fell a mile when he saw it wasn't you.'

A sheepish smile spread over Marta's

thin face. 'Really?' She bit her lip and her pale eyes shone.

Sister French was in the passage as the two second-year students came jauntily through the swing doors to report for duty. She paused on the threshold of her office, watching, as deep in conversation they hurried to hang up their cloaks. With a nod of satisfaction she settled herself at her desk and considered Nurses Westcott and Macbride. The girls had acquitted themselves well, their old feud clearly past and over. Soon she would be preparing their assessment reports for Miss Johnson, and the New Year would see fresh second-year faces replacing these two on Grenville as Westcott and Macbride move back into Block to consolidate in classroom and lecture theatre the work they had done on Grenville.

After the morning's report, Sister deployed her staff and settled down to some paperwork before Sir Freddy Blair's round. She closed her door and sent up a hopeless little prayer for half an hour without interruption. In the ward, Staff Phillips was overseeing the student nurses in their usual routine.

Hannah was much too busy to keep watching out for Jon. But he was there all the while in the back of her mind, and when in a momentary lull she pictured him, striding into the ward with Sir Freddy and his acolytes, her spine tingled with anticipation.

Julie, the young first-year nurse, had been assigned the task of manning the records trolley, and Hannah considered contriving a swap so that she'd be the one to trail around behind the medics and gaze her fill upon Dr Jon. Perhaps even intercept another of those conspiratorial winks, or a brush of the fingers as they handed across patients case-notes.

Pete made a beeline for her side. 'How did you get on, then?' he whispered urgently, running a suspicious eye over Hannah as if he expected to find fang marks on her long and slender neck.

'I'm supposed to be helping Staff with the medicines,' she pointed out firmly. 'If you can make second lunch, I'll tell you all about what it's like to dine with the stars.'

Bea Phillips was poring over the drugs record and Hannah waited patiently at her elbow to double-check every patient's name and prescription. Tablets were scooped into miniature plastic beakers, syrups poured into measured cups. The medicine bottles had been set out on the trolley with labels facing uppermost for quick identification. The two nurses trundled past the bed of a new admission, smiling across at the anxious patient in friendly reassurance.

'Nothing for Mr Colvin,' murmured Bea discreetly, 'till the doctors have seen him. And no solids by mouth for twelve hours.'

'Right, Staff.' Hannah pulled out her pocket notebook and checked on Sister's instructions. 'And pulse and BP to be monitored every half hour.'

'That's it. Dr Harrington saw him about two-thirty today . . . '

'Oh!' murmured Hannah reflectively, knowing Bea was referring to the dawn hours of morning when Hannah lay dreaming of Jon in her sleep. Not sixty minutes since they'd parted.

'Yes,' sighed Bea, 'must have been a busy night. Over there is the other admission — the diabetic. Came in just like a potato crisp, poor fellow. Dr Harrington ordered a litre of normal saline to get fluids into his system fast. Sir Freddy will want to — '

A bellow from further up the ward grabbed their attention. 'Nurse! Nurse! He's going to fall!'

The two nurses sped to the side of a patient six beds away on the far side, tottering by his locker and clutching his chest as he rasped for breath. Onto the bed, pillows stuffed behind his back, soothing words of calm in a moment of crisis.

Out of nowhere appeared Dr Harrington, instantly and quietly taking control. 'That's the way,' Hannah heard his voice murmuring in her left ear. 'Prop him right up. Good girl. Staff! Let's give 40 mg frusemide to clear the oedema from his lungs. And I'll want 250 mg aminophylline for IV injection, Nurse — and make it snappy!'

Hannah rushed for the medicines trolley and grabbed a single-dose container and sterile IV pack, praying he wouldn't notice her shaking hands as she gave him the drug to administer. As the crisis passed Jon remained there chatting to his elderly patient, showing no haste to be on his way as the nurses without further ado carried on with their drugs round.

The back of Hannah's neck seemed to burn from the pressure of his eyes. Yet, whenever she glanced across from beneath her lashes, the doctor's concentration was wholly upon Mr Hacker and it was just a febrile imagination playing tricks. The imprint of his fingers, there just above her elbow, had been real enough, though. Jon had arrived when Hannah was least expecting him, unseen and unheard, and for one blessed moment far from Hannah's thoughts. But now, as she offered sips of water and waited for Dai, the Welshman, to swallow down his variety of pills with the usual complaints about the way everything stuck in his throat, Hannah had a moment to pause and remember with chagrin that reckless accusation she'd hurled at Jon. His lack of sentiment and passion.

In the cold light of day working alongside him on the ward she would never understand how she could have dared.

Hannah dipped her head and concentrated on dosing out her potions and pills.

Pete came loping down the ward to join the Registrar at Mr Hacker's bedside, and Hannah overheard Jon's aside that this patient's chest was pretty bad and that Pete should start him on 28% oxygen immediately.

They were standing by the unlocked

drugs cupboard, counting and double-checking tablets, making sure their numbers tallied with the night staffs record, when Bea and Hannah lifted their heads in surprise to hear voices raised in the main ward.

Next moment, Dr Harrington came storming past like a bull elephant on the rampage, the very antithesis of his usual calm, controlled self.

Bea and Hannah looked at each other, Hannah in alarm, Bea with a what-has-our-beloved-houseman-done-this-time roll of her big brown eyes. Jon didn't keep them long in suspense.

'How the blazes am I supposed to run a medical ward,' he enquired of all and sundry, 'without a peak flow meter?' After him traipsed Pete, shrugging at the startled nurses and miming helplessness with outstretched hands. 'I'll borrow one from another ward, sir!' he was volunteering hopefully. Bea stepped forward to offer assistance, but Jon stormed past as if the plump staff nurse were invisible.

The swing doors rocked on their hinges. It felt as though an electric storm had passed through their midst. 'Phew!' muttered Pete, wiping his sweating forehead with the back of his hand.

'And what was all that about, may I ask?' Sister was standing dazedly at her door, a pair of bifocals resting halfway down her nose.

Bea spoke for all of them, nodding her head with sage understanding. 'Our Dr Jon could do with seeing his bed again. I thought he was looking mighty tired just now. Yes indeed.'

Hannah hesitated, one hand gripping the trolley, the other knuckled against her cheekbones. And I never noticed! she thought. Too much concerned with myself and my own stupid feelings . . .

Pete was demonstrating the state of his nerves by holding out for all to admire a pair of exaggeratedly trembling hands.

The interested face of the medical student peered round his door, looking hopeful. 'Am I missing something good?'

'Back to bed with you, young man!' commanded Sister French, 'or I shall have cotsides put up and pen you in.'

'Shoo!' agreed Pete, brightening as he chivvied Rob back to his room. 'How are you feeling then today?'

Rob scratched his fair, curly head and grimaced. 'Oh, pretty feeble still, I guess. Bored. Fed up. How about sending in Nurse Macbride to special me? We could play chess. Or something.' He grinned up at the houseman who was regarding him with folded arms and an amused and sceptical eye.

'You'll be lucky, mate!'

Pete's lugubrious face suddenly perked up. 'Fancy her then, do you, our magnetic Marta?'

Robert looked pleased beneath the slowly fading jaundice. 'I should say so. Is that what they call her? Magnetic Marta?'

'Something like that.' Pete checked his fingernails with a beatific smile. 'But if you're so bored, young man, I'd

268

suggest catching up on current affairs.' He prodded the newspapers littered across Rob Gilmore's green coverlet. 'Trouble with us medics, we become insular, shut away in our own little empires.' That sounded good, thought Pete. Just the sort of thing the boss might say. He was quite enjoying having Rob on the ward to show off to.

'Heard Imperator Harrington giving you the rocket just now,' laughed Rob Gilmore, climbing into bed. 'Mighty impressive guy, isn't he? Sister tells me he's one of the finest doctors she's ever worked with — brilliant, but can't stand incompetents. Not meaning you, Pete,' he added hastily as the houseman loomed menacingly over his patient. 'No way. I wouldn't be in your shoes for all the tea in China. When I'm doing my house jobs I hope I get Registrars with satisfactory love lives.'

Pete looked astonished. 'What on earth do you know about my boss's love life?'

Gilmore brandished a folded copy of

the *Mail*. 'It's a poor photograph, very grainy and blurred. But tell me, is that or is that not Dr Harrington, glaring grimly as his bird flies off into the night with that actor fellow, Marcus Shero?'

'Let me see that!' Pete snatched the newspaper and whipped it across to the window. Hell's bells! No wonder Big Boy was behaving like a wounded bull elephant! Hold on though. What was this? 'NEW SHEROINE FOR SHERO . . . top model Camilla leaves Langan's Brasserie on the arm of Marcus Shero, while her ex-boyfriend, Dr Jonathan Boyd-Harrington, makes off into the night with his new mystery love.'

New mystery love . . . ? With screwed-up eyes Pete peered intently at the indistinct picture. He whistled through his teeth. That was Hannah all right! Standing close by Harrington as the two of them watched Marcus and Camilla climbing into the actor's waiting Rolls.

Pete set his long lean jaw in an uncharacteristic mood of ill-humour.

Nurse 'Beauty' Westcott had better come up with a mighty plausible reason for being out with Jon Harrington when she was supposed to be dining alone with Shero. He ran his hands through his hair, certain he must be hallucinating; wasn't the arrogant Registrar the last man on earth one might expect to see photographed in the company of a Hanoverian student nurse? And wasn't Hannah's dislike of such an autocratic doctor too genuine to be a mere cover for the secrets of her heart?

Gradually the news percolated into every corner of the great hospital. 'I simply don't believe it!' snapped Sister Junor, reiterating the consensus of opinion. A Senior Registrar taking a second-year student nurse to dinner at Langan's Brasserie? If Miss Johnson had eloped with one of the charge nurses it couldn't have caused more shocking vibrations — particularly when Grace considered how on numerous occasions she'd made it perfectly plain *she* was willing and available. But to be turned down in preference for a silly girl who'd almost got herself killed last month — why, that was worse than insulting!

Ellen French picked up the newspaper from the floor where Junor had tossed it. She wouldn't dream, of course, of saying so; but she was perhaps the only one not entirely surprised. Certain incidents on Grenville had suggested undercurrents of emotion linking nurse and Registrar. But it would be tantamount to pouring petrol on an open fire to mention such a thing while Junor was still quivering with outrage at getting nowhere with the compelling Dr Harrington.

That night Hannah stayed in her room, sick to death of having to explain that no, she was not Dr Harrington's date; that she'd been invited out by Mr Shero to discuss *Beauty and the Beast*. That Dr Harrington as a matter of convenience had driven her back to the Hanoverian while Mr Shero, as a matter of convenience, had escorted

Camilla back to her flat. That it was just the paparazzi trying to stir things up on a slow news night.

'And none of you noticed the photographer? Didn't hear any flash-bulbs popping?' questioned an amused Mango.

'I don't think so.' Hannah wrung her agonised hands. 'How on earth can I ever face Dr Harrington again? He must be cursing me for drawing him into such an embarrassing situation.'

'I don't see why,' insisted Mango reasonably, 'since none of this is your fault. And you've got a perfectly rational explanation to satisfy the nosey parkers. As for the outside world, I can't think who could identify you from such a blurred news-photo.'

One person certainly could — Helen Markland. Astonished to pick out the person of her sister in such celebrated company, she rang that evening to find out what that young lady was up to this time. Groaning, Hannah churned out her hundredth repeat, promising to spend her next day off in Hampstead. 'Helen, I'll come over Friday if that's okay with you. I guess there's lots to tell you since I got back at the end of October.'

'I must confess I'm still mystified. Will you stay the night?'

'Yes, please.' said Hannah gratefully. It wasn't far to travel, but it would be a blessed relief to get away from the hospital environs for a short while.

Next morning Hannah steeled herself to seek out Dr Harrington. It was desperately important to let him know how deeply she regretted everything, all the fuss and gossip about the two of them, so unfounded. His reaction must be faced.

As luck would have it, she'd been down to the path lab with an urgent sample for analysis when, turning the corner of a wide and echoing corridor, she spied Jonathan Harrington, still quite a distance away but heading in her direction.

There were others about. Hannah bit

her lip. She'd intended speaking to him, if she could manage it, somewhere more private. This would only add fuel to the embers of speculation she'd tried so fervently to douse. But Jon had seen her, and their eyes locked fast as he strode inexorably closer. Hannah's face went right out of control, lighting up at the sight of him with all the subtlety of a visual display screen.

She composed herself into some semblance of calm, but her eyes were agonised. Jon's expression was unreadable, unsmiling. Would he ever smile at her again? 'I — I've been wanting to find you . . . ' she began. Jon's eyebrow quirked and he stared at her down the length of that aggressive, broken nose that gave his face such arrogance. 'Yes,' stammered Hannah, her head trembling on a neck that had gone stiff with tension. 'I really must apologise. It must be horribly embarrassing for you — everyone misunderstanding that awful photo!'

Jon had planted himself directly in

her path, making no attempt to avoid her, apparently unconcerned with the curious eyes of passers by. He folded his arms and considered her statement as if the problem had been far from his mind.

'It wasn't a good print, I agree.'

Hannah's dipped head lifted warily.

'Better of Camilla and Marcus. You and I were very blurred.' The hard mouth flickered into a half-smile that melted the last of Hannah's fears. But the sardonic gleam now brightening that lofty eye quickened the dawning suspicion that yet again she was being teased.

She waited for Jon to nod and pass on, but he was shoving his hands into his trouser pockets, pushing aside the white medical coat and almost dislodging his stethoscope so that it hung precariously, poised for a fall. Automatically Hannah stretched forward to help — but Jon's reflexes were faster than hers as he tucked the instrument safely away, leaving her hands to flutter aimlessly in mid-air.

'I knew you were bound to be upset,' she struggled on, though the effort of stringing two cogent words together seemed more arduous than scaling the Himalayas.

'Upset?' he queried.

'Because of what people were saying.'

'No one has said anything to *me*. What were people saying?'

He was teasing her now, challenging the forthright, determined Hannah Westcott to live up to her own reputation of speaking out at all times.

For the first time in her life, Hannah chickened out. She didn't believe for a moment that he didn't know: and she wasn't about to gratify that perverted sense of humour by relating all those comments about Jon being her . . . she being his . . .

'I'm needed back on the ward, Doctor,' she said with stiff pride.

'Then tell that goon of a boyfriend of yours that if he hasn't found me a peak flow meter by this afternoon I shall have his guts for garters.'

This really got Hannah's goat. If she couldn't stand up for *herself*, she could certainly put in a strong word in Pete's defence. 'Dr Harrington!' she said firmly, with a tilt of the Westcott chin and a furl of Julie Christie underlip, her challenging eyes on a level with the bleep clipped on to the Registrar's breast pocket, 'Dr Fuller is *not* a goon. He takes a serious professional attitude to medicine.'

Jon Harrington's mouth made a wry grimace. 'That is a statement, Nurse, that I shall be delighted to see proven. I fear, however, that a girlfriend is hardly an unbiased counsel — '

' — I am *not* Pete's girlfriend!' Hannah could have stamped her size-six foot, she was so annoyed. How many more times?

Now she has denied him thrice, thought Jon, grinning secretly as he gazed down at the top of Nurse Westcott's quivering cap. Dear stubborn Hannah — champion of the underdog — perhaps she really means it?

He shot his cuff to check his watch and Hannah saw that instantly she was dismissed from his thoughts. Preoccupation with matters of life and death once more claimed priority: Jon was not seeing her now — though she stood but three feet away from him. She doubted if he'd even heard her last vehement protest. But he'd certainly been obliged to hear out her praise of Dr Fuller's solemn commitment to his calling.

So let me down if you dare, Pete Fuller, threatened Hannah, staring after Dr Harrington with clenched fists and head drawn back. Let me down — if you dare!

9

'If the painters hadn't left that newspaper behind, Hannie dear, I shouldn't have known a thing about it.'

In response, Hannah shrugged ruefully and linked her hands behind her head, staring at pictures in the blazing log fire. If you looked hard enough there were mysterious caverns and weird, magical images . . .

Helen twitched creamy Victorian lace across the window bay and shut out the snowy Hampstead streets from view. The portable telephone shrilled and gold bracelets jangled about her fine-boned wrist as she leaned across to answer its call. Her tranquil madonna face was instantly transformed with joy. 'Bram! Darling, where are you?'

Four months pregnant and radiant with it. Hannah found herself wondering what it was like, and if she would

280

look half as super, be a fraction as happy. Such speculation was not her usual style. But lately she'd been unable to contain her meandering thoughts — and they inevitably flowed back to one impossible man.

'That was Bram,' announced her sister unnecessarily. 'What a good thing I've got you to keep me company tonight. It's snowing a blizzard up in Edinburgh, so he's staying the night with one of the university professors.'

'How did his lecture go?' Helen's surgeon-husband was notorious for his disregard for sartorial matters. 'I hope you packed him matching socks.'

Her reward was a playful tap on the head with a newspaper carefully folded at the picture under discussion. 'Very well, *thank* you. He's an excellent speaker, is my darling Bram.' Helen plonked herself down beside her sister and took up her knitting, blonde hair twisted into a silky knot on the top of her elegant head, her tall and usually-slender body snugly clad in a peach-pink velour track suit. 'Hey! I recognise that skirt, don't I?'

'Your cast-off mini, no less. Quite a respectable length on *me*, though, wouldn't you say?' Stretching out her black wool legs, Hannah couldn't resist trying to picture them through Jon's eyes: too substantial to compete with Camilla's yard-long limbs! Her appreciative gaze roamed Helen's private den in the luxurious family-sized home. Amber roses out of season. Velvety vanilla carpets. Downy-cushioned chintz chairs. Helen's favourite books and magazines; her faithful sewing machine in permanent situ and ready for action. Bram must be frightfully rich . . . mused Hannah wonderingly. And of course it was all so tidy and well organised; typically Helen. She'd been Gold Medallist nurse of the year, once upon a time, at the Royal Hanoverian.

'And now,' probed Helen, judging the moment was ripe with her sister relaxed and cosily at her ease, 'perhaps you'd care to spill the beans about this new man in your life. I realised Dr Derby must be out of the picture since he suddenly ceased being the main topic of your letters home, but I was under the impression that Philip Fuller was replacing him very nicely.'

'*Pete* Fuller,' corrected Hannah. Somewhat glumly, to her sister's way of thinking. 'He's just a friend, like I told you over supper when we were talking about *Beauty and the Beast*.'

'Bram and I must come and see you in that,' said Helen enthusiastically. 'I never got farther than the front row of the chorus. They seemed to prefer my legs to my voice. Once I had to wear a big white tee-shirt and black tights and stiletto heels.'

'Oh, I remember you telling us,' interrupted Hannah. 'On the front it said SAUCY, and on the back — BUT QUITE OK. Mum was a bit shocked, but there — she's led a sheltered life.'

Helen was stoking the fire, carefully placing a log so it wouldn't roll out of the grate and send sparks on to the rug.

'This picture of you in the *Mail on Sunday*,' she prompted.

'Oh hell, the parents didn't see it . . . ?'

'I'm sure we'd have heard by now if they'd started reading the tabloids,' said Helen calmly. 'I've been doing a bit of research myself — or rather Bram has. Apparently you were with Jonathan Boyd-Harrington, no less, who is particularly well regarded by Sir Freddy Blair.'

'I could have told you all that,' said Hannah, rather crossly because she was feeling distinctly uncomfortable now. What else had Bram dragged up? Jon's affair with Camilla, no doubt. And big sister was working up to a lecture.

'And does he plan, do you think, to marry you?' asked Helen, pinning her younger sister with that clear blue scrutiny that had brought Bram Markland to his knees.

The question brought such a look of horror to her sister's agonised face that Helen frowned in confusion. 'Look, dear, just what is going on? It's obvious you're eating your heart out over someone. And if it isn't Dickie or Pete, then I'm assuming you and Jon — '

'I should be so lucky,' muttered Hannah gloomily, twisting in her fingers a strand of Helen's white baby wool. Who else, though, would hear her out with such sympathy? Solely take her part? . . . With tears in her eyes, Hannah let the heartrending tale come pouring out. Putting into words — at last — with such overwhelming relief, the saga of her relationship with Jon Harrington, right from that day they first met in France. Owning up to the knowledge that a future without him seemed empty of happiness — ridiculous though that might seem when he was engaged to someone else. Admitting she was struggling in the throes of a hopeless case of Love. Love, with a huge great painful L . . .

Helen was giving little nods of understanding that said wordlessly, I've been there too . . . falling in love with an impossible man. Or so it seemed at the time. Hannah, realising suddenly that she was raking up an old anguish for her sister, felt even more wretched. But it had worked out for Helen, hadn't it? . . . Might there perhaps be a glimmer of hope on the distant horizon?

The half-finished jacket for her baby lay abandoned on the arm of Helen's chair. She thought for some moments about what she had heard, then said with gentle good sense that there must have been misunderstandings between her sister and the Registrar all along the line. 'Besides, Hannie, if he supposes you're his houseman's girlfriend, what can he do other than make a dignified retreat? From what you say, it seems to me the two of you are edging round a circle of attraction. He's made the moves, but you've unwittingly rebuffed him every time. I suspect you've been playing Joan of Arc — yet again! Why can't Peter Fowler fight his own battles? Jon Harrington may not *realise* you have this tendency to leap into the fray on behalf of life's victims. He must suppose you're backing up your boy-friend, Dr Fowler.'

'Fuller,' corrected Hannah with a sigh. Yes, it made sense. Why couldn't she have worked that out for herself, it sounded so reasonable? She supposed it was a case of the onlooker seeing more of the game. 'But three *times* he's questioned me about Pete. And every time I've insisted Pete Fuller is not my boyfriend.'

With her sweet, pacifying smile, Helen poured soothing oil on the troubled waters of her sister's love life. 'Then you may well have convinced him the third time. But knowing you as well as I do, Hannie, you've always been impulsive. And you sometimes let your tongue run away with you.' Helen was judging her moment. Bram had unearthed a well-kept secret about one Dr Jonathan Harrington, a secret that would soon be known to the world. For Camilla was about to marry. And her bridegroom would not be Jon . . .

'You know me *too* well!' With a sheepish smile Hannah continued, 'Want me to tell you what I christened Dr Jon?'

'Clearly you're rather proud of it. Go on.'

The wind went out of Hannah's sails. She bit her lip in shame. 'Dr Beast,' she volunteered miserably.

'But I thought you were supposed to be his number one admirer!' Helen's blue eyes conveyed such gentle reproof that Hannah shrank into herself with shoulders hunched. Not so clever now, are you, Westcott? her conscience chided. You've been your own worst enemy.

'Sounds to me as if Jon Harrington might have picked up the idea you don't much like him.'

Hannah's throat constricted with agony. Jon was so attractive and clever that in truth she'd been scared of him, over-awed. In self-protection she had pretended indifference: but she'd acted

288

too well, had overplayed her part. Been defensive and rude, in a manner quite alien to her natural temperament — justified, she'd convinced herself, by Jon's blatant interference in her love affair with Dr Derby. And like an idiot she'd allowed herself to fall in love with such a totally impossible man.

Helen was more right than she knew. There'd been that day when Hannah had said to Jon's face that she *hated* him! knowing full well that the opposite was true.

'Oh, Helen!' She buried her head in her hands. 'Jon's going to marry Camilla — and she doesn't love him like I do. *Nobody* could. And he doesn't love her either. Put it down to female intuition if you like, but I'm certain of it.'

'Calm down, calm down. Through Bram's contacts we happen to have discovered something else about the Jon-Camilla business. So calm yourself, and listen to me carefully.'

Pete was feeling rather pleased with himself. Hannah's suggestion that he should each morning write out a list of all the tasks he must get through, crossing off each job the minute it was completed, had kept him out of trouble with the boss for more than a week. In fact, Dr Harrington had been pleasantly complimentary over the way he'd handled a potentially tricky situation on one of the women's medical wards. And Sister Susan Wycliffe, who was young and pretty and in her first post in charge, had definitely been giving Pete the eye. This put an extra jauntiness in Dr Fuller's step. It might be interesting to date a more mature woman of twenty-four. Of late Hannah had been strangely withdrawn. Something was biting her. Perhaps it was just the extra strain of so many evening rehearsals on top of a busy day on the ward. The panto loomed ever nearer.

Pete got out his notepad and added

Harrington's latest dictat to his list. You had to admit it: the Registrar was a demanding sort of cuss, but he took his teaching commitment towards junior doctors seriously and you learned a hell of a lot from him. Tomorrow afternoon, for example, he wanted all junior medical staff in for a practical workshop on cardio-pulmonary resuscitation techniques: to check that they could all deal competently with patients having heart attacks. There'd been a lot of hoo-ha in the press recently over the inefficiency of hospital doctors in such crises — even though they'd all been taught resuscitation back in med school.

Grinning to himself, Pete added a neat full-stop to the brief reminder in his notebook. One female houseman — trust a woman! — had the temerity to protest to Harrington that they'd done this sort of thing right at the beginning of their medical courses.

'With videos and playbacks . . . and demonstration inflatable dummies?' questioned Dr Harrington blandly, with a sardonic lift of his expressive black eye-brows.

She'd soon shut up, after a murmur of, 'Oh well, perhaps not quite as thoroughly . . . but I feel confident I — er . . . ' Pete had grinned as her words trailed into hesitancy. He'd whispered unsympathetically into her ear when the Registrar's attention was diverted, 'Better be dead good, mate, or you'll be the one under arrest! I dare say we're all confident of the *theory* — but he's talking about saving lives. Regular practical sessions are vital. Good for Hannah's Dr Beast!' Pete felt in his pocket for his paper of lists. No pen, though. He'd note down the day and time soon as he got back to his room. Organisation Man Mark Two, Dr Pete Fuller.

True enough, Hannah *was* feeling dejected. And the rehearsals were in full spate with the performance just a week away, so she was extra tired. That revelation about Jon and Camilla had seemed like a bombshell, a miracle. But nothing had happened. She never saw Jon with less than half a dozen others in tow. Occasionally with Marcus Shero. No chance to tell him how deeply she regretted her defensive stance of the past. Helen had said he sounded very protective rather than interfering! That Hannah was taking independence a shade too far . . .

Hannah felt she'd grown up over-night, and a very painful process it had proved. How, she wondered miserably, did you convey that to the man you loved? Tell him you were madly and irrevocably devoted to him? grateful for any crumb that might fall your way, in spite of all appearances to the contrary.

Her moods escalated between pinnacles of joy at learning that he was after all a free agent; the depths of hopelessness when she convinced herself it was her vivid imagination that had deceived her into thinking Jon could have even the smallest feeling for her.

It's impossible! agonised Hannah,

remembering Jon and his retinue progressing down the ward with never a glance in her direction as she hovered, yearning to meet for an instant the dark regard that sent shivers down her spine. Surely I must have convinced him there's nothing romantic between me and Pete? In novels I'd have only to capture his eyes with my own pleading gaze and he'd read the truth therein. I'd whisper something like, 'I *understand* about you and Camilla. How you've gallantly protected her from the media, her and her tennis star husband-to-be, until she's ready for the world to know the secret of her real-life love affair. Acted as her decoy lover . . . '

'Are you with us, Nurse, or are you perhaps dwelling in the realms of fantasy?'

Hannah's lower lip caught between her teeth as she realised that Sister French had had to ask her twice to take the plate she was holding out as she presided over the hot dinner trolley. 'Minced chicken for Mr Gilmore. And I shall be glad when this pantomime is over and done with — you're looking quite washed out these days.'

'Yes, Sister. Sorry, Sister,' mumbled Hannah, and fled away with the warm plate of food. Marta intercepted her at the bottom of the ward. 'Go on, Westcott, let me take that in for him.' Later, in the canteen, Marta told Hannah her secret. The two girls didn't usually get the same lunch break, but both Sister and Staff Phillips were on and the ward was over the busy morning rush.

'But that's marvellous, Macbride. So long as your own family won't be too disappointed at your being invited to Robert Gilmore's for Christmas. I didn't realise he was being discharged so soon.' Quite a number of the less ill patients would be allowed home for the festival, but Gilmore would not be coming back. It had, after all, been a mild bout of hepatitis and he was fast regaining his strength.

'I haven't got a family. I was brought

up in a children's home.' Marta shrugged this off as though the deprivation were of no consequence — but Hannah felt awful inside. Poor Marta, she thought in distress. We could have been so much kinder and shown more understanding. But how lovely that she's made such a hit with this medical student. Pete had said the chap seemed quite besotted . . .

'I'm very happy indeed for you,' said Hannah warmly, her eyes speaking for her in their glowing greeny depths. If only we could all be as happy, she thought. It never occurred to her that it was Marta who had kept silent when they asked for volunteers to work at Christmas. That it was Hannah, with a family who would deeply miss her and of whom she would be thinking all over Christmas, who had jumped in and given her name. And Marta Macbride, with no particular concern whether she worked or not (for at the time she had not even been aware of young Gilmore's existence), had maintained a sullen silence until pressed to offer her services to cover the New Year.

It never occurred to Hannah, either, that life wasn't fair when it rewarded selfish people like Macbride with luck in love, when for life's true carers things seemed to go hopelessly wrong. She stiffened her back and straightened her shoulders and determined to look on the bright side. If people were beginning to notice she was downhearted then the time had certainly come to pull herself together and not depress others with a self-pitying, long face.

'When can we decorate the ward?' she asked Sister at the beginning of the afternoon session when they had reviewed the morning and organised their work for the rest of the day shift.

'Ooh ye/s!' enthused young Julie, the first-year. 'I can't wait to put up the Christmas decorations!'

Sister looked enquiringly at her staff nurse. 'Shall we make it the beginning of next week, do you think, Bea? I can't remember when we tackled it last year.

There's a big cardboard box on the top shelf at the back of the linen cupboard, and all the tree decorations are in the bottom drawer of that filing cabinet.'

'I expect they'll bring us a Christmas tree on Saturday,' Bea pointed out. 'Monday would be a good day, when there's no clinical teaching on the ward.'

'Right then, that's settled.' The nurses filed out into the ward to deal with bottles and guided tours to the lavatories before the men had their afternoon nap. Hannah was just coming out of the sluice when Dr Fuller came jauntily through the ward doors, arms swinging and whistling a snappy number from *Beauty and the Beast*.

'You're looking pleased with yourself,' smiled Hannah. 'Is it the prospect of moving on to pastures new?'

Pete held up superstitiously crossed fingers. 'If I can just keep my nose clean till the New Year. It's a shame that you have to go just when you're beginning to feel on top of the job. In a way I'll be sorry to be coming off Sir Freddy's firm. Your Dr Beast has made a better doctor of me!' He crackled the paper of handwritten lists in his coat pocket. 'One more blood-letting job for Organisation Man. Mr Glossop, new patient, lead me to him.'

'Oh yes,' said Hannah, 'the patient with GOK.'

'That's the one — in for a whole battery of tests. Jon wants the results yesterday, as usual,' added Pete with a wryly cynical smile. 'And I aim to keep in his good books till our parting moment. Hey, guess what I suggested to him this morning — or rather told him it was your idea.'

Hannah raised a nervous hand to check the back of her neck for wandering strands of newly-shampooed hair. 'What are you talking about, Pete?'

'They're doing the panto posters and I told our Jon you thought it should be called *Nurse Beauty and Doctor Beast.*'

Her face went pale. 'Pete, you idiot! What could be more tactless! You know very well he overheard me call *him* that. Oh, Pete, how *could* you?'

Pete was startled. Hannah looked on the verge of tears and was clearly very distressed by his harmless bit of teasing. He put an arm about her shoulders, but whipped it away when he saw Sister French coming down the passage with her cloak on. 'Of course I didn't,' he hissed out of the corner of his mouth. 'I only wanted to make you laugh!' He waved his list at Sister to impress her with his efficiency. 'Okay if I disturb Martin Glossop for a blood test, Sister?'

'Why not?' said Ellen French with an astute glance at Nurse Westcott's damp eyes. 'Anything's better than having you disturb my nurses.' Pete sprang to open the door for her and exhaled noisily when she was safely out of earshot. 'Drat and double-drat! What's the odds she reports me to Jon for dishonourable conduct?' He patted his pockets in a vain search for something to mop Hannah's brimming eyes, but she had disappeared into the sluice and came back punishing her nose with a piece of tissue. 'Pre-menstrual, are we?' he enquired knowingly.

'Take a running jump, Doctor!' was the smart riposte.

Three minutes later a sudden yell from across the ward brought Hannah's head up with a start. She'd been checking the dressing on Mr Hawtry's varicose ulcer — just across from where Pete was supposed to be dealing with the mystery ailments of Mr Glossop — who now slumped ashen-faced in the high-back chair, face white as a hospital sheet, legs sticking out like a wooden toy soldier's.

Hannah and Pete heaved the poor man on to the counterpane and jerked the flowery curtains to enclose Mr Glossop's bed. 'Red, it appears, is not his favourite colour,' muttered Pete. 'Mr Glossop begrudges me even one drop of his blood.' He rolled a frustrated eye at the nurse poised on the other side of the bed, who grimaced in sympathy. It did happen from time to time — a patient so phobic that he collapsed at the approach of a needle.

'I've got to get some blood from him — got to. Simple as that. It's his blood or mine.'

'Shush, Pete!' reproved Hannah as the patient's eyelids flickered. 'Mr Glossop,' she said with kindly concern, 'you've terrified Dr Fuller, fainting on him like that! He'll be scared to come near this ward from now on.'

But Martin Glossop was not to be chivvied into the trace of a smile. 'Good job too,' he muttered, keeping Pete in check with suspicious eye. All the same he was not averse to having his hand stroked by such a pretty girl, her face all peachy concern, and framed within an aureole of soft little waves. 'Just a little prick, a wee sample of your blood for the doctor's tests. It won't take a moment. There — your colour's coming back now, you must be feeling so much better.'

Mr Glossop couldn't resist Hannah. He ignored the houseman and began telling her about his family and his work as a computer salesman, how he'd always been funny about blood and needles. Hannah reached over to push up the left pyjama sleeve so Pete could move in with a deft syringe. But Martin Glossop wasn't kidding: his face altered dramatically as though the doctor's long-chinned humorous countenance might be that of Dracula himself, hot-foot from the forests of Transylvania.

'I always faint. Been like it all my life,' he announced with gloomy satisfaction.

'Just look at me while the doctor does it,' advised Hannah. 'I'll keep talking and, before you know, it'll all be over. He's very good — you'll hardly feel a thing.'

It was a nice try, but Mr Glossop had worked himself into such a state his veins had knotted like salt-weathered rope. It was twenty minutes later that Pete dashed into the treatment room with a suggestion of precious red in his test tube. Julie the first-year was there, lackadaisically unpacking the dressing and treatment packs which each day were sent up to the wards from the central sterilising department. Her face brightened at the sight of Pete: he was such a tease, creeping up and tickling you and making you shriek with fright when Sister wasn't looking.

Hannah whizzed in and out again in seconds. 'Mr Glossop wants to throw up now.'

'So do I,' muttered Pete.

'What are you doing?' said Julie nosily, sidling over to watch.

Pete treated the enquiry as seriously as he imagined his Registrar would do. The girl seemed genuinely interested, so he explained the purpose of the test and how it would help this particular patient's diagnosis.

'Why are you doing it here on the ward, then?'

'I'm in a bit of a hurry, Julie.'

'You're terribly clever, Pete,' murmured Julie, eyes a-twinkle, her fingers dancing up the back of his white coat as he bent tensely over the work surface.

Pete couldn't help smiling. 'You're terribly clever, Pete,' he mimicked in a little-girlish voice. He straightened up swilling the pathetic sample of crimson in the bottom of the glass tube. Three mils at a pinch! — and that guy carrying on as though he was being callously exsanguinated. Julie lost interest and wandered away to count packs of syringes.

Pete put the sample back in the test tube rack and reached for a pipette which he set down on the sink's stainless steel draining board. He blew down the glass out of habit, and with far more care and caution than was his wont, lowered the graduated rod into that unutterably precious sample, steadily drawing up the precious two mils he needed for testing.

Julie was just thinking to herself that a sprig of mistletoe dangling over the sink would be just the excuse for getting to grips with Pete. She made a mental note to bring some in, and, with a sparkle in her button-brown eyes, lips compressed against a spurt of giggles, she tiptoed across to the houseman's stooping figure. To get her own back for all Pete's teasing.

'Wheee!' Two index fingers dove wickedly into his unsuspecting ribcage.

'Aaagh!' gagged Pete, the precious sample backfiring over walls, floor and sink, and polka-dotting his white coat with red.

Hannah, in the doorway, gripped her tray of thermometers and gaped in sheer horror. The blood they'd sweated over for at least twenty minutes!

All that was left of Julie was the rush of air in the wake of her fleeing skirts. 'Um . . . sorry, Pete. I think I'm needed on the — '

Hannah leaned against the wall and began helplessly to giggle. Well, what else could you do but see the funny side of it? When life got so unbearable and every blessed thing went wrong . . . her hiccups threatened to gallop right into rampant hysteria.

Pete, with ribs still stinging, grinned and ruefully stroked his lean jaw. Then he too succumbed to yelps of riotous laughter.

And this was the sight that greeted Sister French and Dr Harrington as they strode into the splattered treatment room — Fuller and Westcott writhing in paroxysms of totally incomprehensible mirth.

'In my office at once, Nurse.' Sister's voice betrayed no more emotion than a judge passing sentence.

Dr Harrington, however, was clearly containing himself by an extreme effort of will. 'We were expecting you, *Doctor*,' he ground out in a growl rich with sarcasm, 'at the resuscitation workshop.' He folded his arms and his contemptuous eye included Hannah along with her accomplice.

Pete struck his forehead with a groan. 'I put it on my list for *tomorrow*. I couldn't be more sorry, sir. I was really looking forward to that. I reckon we could do with the revision.' Hannah, in all innocence since she had played no part in the fiasco, was hovering anxiously, not wanting to make Sister any crosser, but feeling honour-bound to get a word in in Pete's defence. Sister was still there in the doorway, her hands on her hips, slowly shaking her head as she examined her once pristine white-tiled treatment room.

'Sister . . . Dr Harrington — it wasn't Pete . . . er . . . Dr Fuller's fault. I'm afraid that — '

'Come!' commanded the older nurse with the coldest imaginable expression in her disappointed brown eyes. She stood aside, and there was nothing Hannah could do but obey that ominous command. Poor Pete — and that accident hadn't been his fault. If they only *knew* the struggle to get a sample of Mr Glossop's blood, it would be pats on the back they'd be handing out instead of scalpels levelled at the jugular!

The doctors had disappeared when Hannah set to with a cloth and a bucket of soapy suds to clear up all the mess. Now that she was in everyone's bad books and had further reduced herself in Jon Harrington's eyes, it should have seemed like the end of the world. But Hannah was almost past caring. She sloshed water on to the floor and swabbed away with all the vigour she could muster. One thing about nursing, you were much too busy to mope!

Suddenly a small pair of pigeon-toed black lace-up shoes appeared within two feet of Hannah's nose. She stopped dreaming that her cloth was a Brillo pad and that it was Dr Beast's broad, insensitive back that she was punishing for its cruel indifference to her broken heart. 'Julie! I could throttle you, you little pest!' she snapped.

Julie was shaking with fright, poor kid, fearful that she had got Pete into the most terrible trouble with Dr Harrington. Which she most probably had, pointed out Hannah sternly, with all the authority and experience of the well-into-her-second-year to a quivering member of the PTS.

'You and Pete won't tell on me, will you? Oh, please don't tell Sister what I did!' Julie was desperately sorry that her thoughtless bit of fun had turned out so badly, swearing she had learned her lesson and would take nursing more seriously in future. 'If I fail my Assignment they'll put me back a set, and I won't be with my friends,' she wailed.

'And what about the mess you've got poor Dr Fuller into?' demanded Hannah, sitting back on her haunches and resting her wet hands on her plastic apron. 'Why should I save your skin if you're only nursing because you can't think of anything else to do in life? Out there,' Hannah pointed an indignant finger towards the world on the other side of the window, 'are hundreds of girls, born nurses, just longing to come and train at a place as good as the Royal Hanoverian.'

'I know,' stuttered Julie, 'and I'm truly sorry. I know I mess about a bit, but I won't from now on.'

'You'd better not,' scolded Hannah, 'because I warn you, I'll be keeping my eye on you. And if you give me the least cause I shall certainly tell.'

'Oh, you are a brick, Westcott! I do think you're one of the nicest nurses in the whole place. And I promise I won't try and get off with your boyfriend again.'

'Oh, get away with you,' muttered Hannah, and when alone once more she renewed her scrubbing and scouring with a vengeance, pretending in her vivid imagination that she was really a bird and that it was possible to fly out of that window and up into the skies, so high she could take herself right out of the world and all of its foolish misunderstanding.

10

Damn the man! . . . From his vantage point in the shadows Jon gritted his teeth, observing Marcus as he directed Hannah's movements in this very important scene with the Beast. The girl's eyes were focused exclusively upon the famous face downturned to hers; her hands enclasped between the actor's, her whole expression rapt with concentration. And something else, judged Jon, fuming with irritation. He'd managed to sabotage that dinner-date à deux. But just how deeply were these two involved? And was Shero the reason for Dr Fuller's unsuccessful pursuit of Nurse Westcott? when — and no accounting for their taste! — he was apparently something of a heart-throb among the student nurses?

Harrington's jawline was taut and grim. He felt himself responsible for that slip of a girl in the circle of light. But for him, those two would never have met. And Marcus might be an old friend, but Jon had never approved of the actor's ladykilling ways. If that reprobate Dick Derby hadn't been deserving of such a lovable creature, then no more was Marcus. Yet who could have predicted that so sophisticated and worldly a man might find a young student nurse quite as enticing?

. . . *damn* the fellow, kissing her cheek like that in front of the whole cast — including young Fuller, who looked as if he'd just been kicked in the gut. My good friend Shero, seethed the Registrar, his eyes opaque with impotent fury.

Marcus had no qualms about winding up his audience; it was an art in which he excelled. Inside he was chortling. Jon's a stubborn man. But iron wills are made to crack . . . 'Your sister is correctly informed,' he whispered into Hannah's shell-like ear, 'an affair of convenience rather than an affaire de coeur. I was planning to let you in on the secret myself. Be bold. Ask him to marry you! You're just the sort of good girl that man needs. I've been rooting for you right from the start. See, Jon's watching us like a hawk. He's absolutely livid with jealousy!'

Ask Jon Harrington to . . . The very idea!

Her breathing came raggedly in deep gasps, as if Hannah had run a mile. So much she longed to believe every encouraging word. But words were no proof: and greatly as she admired Marcus, he possessed such a clever, silken tongue. Hannah's eyes were cloudy with doubt, and she was hardly aware of Marcus's celebrated lips brushing against her cheek, the hands sliding up her arms, bare in the skimpy white tee-shirt. Yet there was this desperate need to convince herself that in the secret recesses of his proud and fortressed heart Jon could truly feel something akin to love for her.

Meanwhile in the dark body of the rehearsal room Jon continued to smart in that unaccustomed state of powerlessness. Much more of *that* and the whole company would believe Shero and Nurse Westcott had embarked on a steamy new affair! And it wasn't five minutes since her name had been linked with his own. Not that Marcus would give a fig for Hannah's reputation. While he, Jonathan Harrington, must continue to behave — because of that infuriating gutter-press picture — as if she was a nurse and not a woman.

Jon grabbed a copy of the script and forced his thunder-colour eyes to concentrate on the text. To let a girl like that know the extent of his feelings would be unkind and unfair, for she was so obviously the marrying kind: warm-hearted and caring and with all the values of a sincere and honest person. And Jon was not in the market for marriage — and never would be.

He slapped the script down and

strode across to break those two up.

'Goodbye, Marcus — and thank you for everything,' Hannah was saying gratefully. 'I wish you didn't have to go.'

'When Broadway summons, one must obey. But remember what I told you, darling. It's all going to work out just fine.'

'What *are* you on about?' snapped Jon, glowering by the actor's side. Need he be quite so abrupt? wondered Hannah, sensing that the doctor was in a rotten mood again. After all, they owed so much to Marcus Shero. Her heart gave a little leap . . . but was she clutching at straws? Over-eager to convince herself that it really was as Marcus said: Dr Harrington exhibiting the clinical signs of *jealousy*.

Her uncertain, questing smile was rewarded with a scowl so profound Hannah's heart plummeted as swiftly as it had leaped an instant before. Of all the men in the world, why did this terrifying, awesome giant have to be the one she'd lost her heart to? What could a slip of a girl do to cure herself of what must surely be the most hopeless case of love that ever existed?

Wistfully Hannah looked back at the group of her friends, a jolly carefree crowd surrounding Pete and the other young doctors, waiting there in the body of the hall to see whether they would be needed to rehearse again, or if they might slope off to the Lamb and Flag. To join them would mean a deliberate choice to walk away from the nearness of Jon. And her feet were unwilling to take her.

Marcus strode with professional confidence into the centre stage, and stood, legs astride, hands on hips, head thrown back and cobra eyes glittering, waiting for the hush that came almost instantly. He wished them all *bonne chance* and farewell.

And he left. The production staff went into a huddle before announcing the end of rehearsal for that night — but would Beauty and the Beast stay on for another ten minutes with Dr

Harrington, to go over the cave scene.

'Right,' called Jon, isolated in the shadows of the now emptied hall. 'We've had the (we hope!) intensive comedy of the Beast's transformation by plastic surgery. He is recuperating in the corner of the cave, when in creeps Beauty, quite unaware of his condition. She weeps bitterly when she sees you, Beast . . . carry on from there, please.'

The Beast was being played by one of the hospital administrators, renowned for his Byronic head of black curls and the regularity of his handsome features, combined with a splendid tenor singing voice. He kept glancing surreptitiously at his watch, for he had a wife and young family back in Kingston and would have preferred to be on his way home.

Hannah pretended to stumble over a drip stand, almost dropping her (imaginary) candle. 'I can't bear to see you like this, Beast!' she sobbed, flinging herself down and caressing the poor bandaged head.

Beast flinches with agony as the drip is wrenched from his arm. 'My bandages — you're soaking them!' he growls.

'Sit up,' directed Jon with an impatient gesture, '*before* you tear them off — and Hannah, get back so the audience can see what he's doing. That's the way. Carry on from there.'

Jon stopped them again when they reached the bit where Hannah's lines went, 'Terrific face — shame about the body.' He persistently criticised her delivery. 'If you laugh, the effect will be undermined. Keep a straight face at all costs. Turn and take a few steps towards the audience, shake your head regretfully as you speak. Don't look round at Gareth.'

At the back of the cave the Beast was energetically stripping off his fur catsuit to reveal the princely outfit he was sporting underneath. At least, he would be on the night.

'You turn — gasp with amazement . . . rub your eyes in disbelief. Rush over into his arms. No, you can't tread there because there'll be a boulder right in your path. We ought to have got this floor marked out to show where the props will go.'

The next bit Hannah found specially embarrassing, since it involved an amorous clinch with her handsome prince. Neither of them was inclined to feel particularly abandoned, not in their everyday clothes anyway. The Muse would inspire everyone on the night of nights.

'What on earth is Jon up to?' muttered Hannah into Gareth's ear. 'Margaret Wise, the pathologist, is supposed to be directing the romantic bits. Your buttons are sticking into my — '

'Sorry,' apologised Gareth, shifting his position to peer across Hannah's head at his watch. 'I say, Jon, would you mind awfully if we called it a day? I've got a train to catch.'

Her partner disappeared, but the doctor wasn't about to let Hannah off the hook. He had found a piece of white chalk and was marking out shapes on the wooden floor of the 'stage' area. 'Let's just test this out,' he suggested, 'with me standing in for Gareth.' With surprising agility for such a powerfully built man, he crouched, then stretched out in the Beast's sleeping pose. Hannah was transfixed. This was totally ludicrous. Her lines had flown right out of her head.

'You'll get filthy down there,' she pointed out, for Jon wasn't dressed for a sprawl on the boards. His slim grey flannels and navy Guernsey were immaculate as you'd expect. He was eyeing Hannah's white tee-shirt, with its emblem of a nurse's cap and stethoscope rampant, her faded denim jeans which she'd shrunk in the bath for the right clinging fit. Clothes which would come to no harm if you were expecting to grovel in a cave.

'The sooner you get on with it, the sooner I'll be up on my feet again,' he pointed out reasonably.

Hannah managed fairly well till she got to 'Terrific face — shame about the body.' She held her head in her hands and just shrieked with laughter. Even Jon was forced to give in to one of his rare transforming smiles. 'Come on,' he protested, springing to his feet and brushing the seat of his trousers, 'you won't have to get hysterics on the night. It's the audience's joke, not yours. Let's get on to the next bit.'

All the laughter drained out of Hannah's system. The next bit. Why? 'But there's no dialogue!'

The doctor shrugged nonchalant shoulders. There was dust on his right arm and Hannah longed to brush it off, but dared not. 'I want us to pace out the action.' He waved her back across the stage into her original position. 'Now run towards me, avoiding the chalk marks, while I count how many strides it takes to get me from here to you.'

He made her do it again, but faster. And again, until Hannah was breathing in gasps. Each time his hands caught her and held her steady against him. Each time he told her to take it just once more, until she stumbled and fell smack into his arms, to be grasped firmly, her cheek against the warm wool of his Guernsey, her arms reaching round to his broad back with a will that was all their own and none of Hannah's doing. It was clear that those arms did not intend to let Jon go. Ever. He didn't seem to be in any particular hurry either, but gathered Hannah up so firmly she was obliged to stand on tiptoe; supporting her against his awesome frame with a closeness that transmitted the warm vitality of flesh and bone and sinew, and the thunder of a vulnerable human heart. There was no apology or do-you-mind as his deliberate mouth claimed hers. He shifted slightly so Hannah could get her arm up and round his neck (in her dreams that arm had just floated into position) to stroke the back of his head and caress that wonderfully thick and waving hair — it was so soft! — as in her wildest fantasies she'd imagined herself doing. Then for the fleetest second they drew breath before resuming that kiss that went on and on . . .

Jon was the first to break apart. With intense fingers he raked back the recalcitrant lock of hair which so intriguingly ruffled his cool persona. Plummeted from elation to dismay, Hannah witnessed the purple-grey eyes lose their fire, become shuttered and remote as they scanned the far reaches of the unlit hall to check that the two of them had been unobserved. Away from his body-heat she was sharply aware of the cold. She crossed her arms and her hands clasped her shoulders, shivering with an emotion strongly resembling the trauma of shock.

Jon walked away from her, strolling over to the piano where her robin-red sweater lay discarded. 'Rehearsal over, Beauty,' he said gently, winding the sleeves about her neck like a woollen scarf. 'But that's the way to play it next Friday night.

Plenty of *passion*. Right? Now you've proved you've got it in you . . . '

And he didn't even wait to see her safely back to base.

*   *   *

The last of the visitors had gone, and the atmosphere in the ward was relaxed and tranquil, the patients looking forward to the arrival of suppers. Hannah should have gone off duty at four, but they'd been too busy to start on the Christmas decorations earlier, so she'd offered to stay on in her own time. Besides, Dr Harrington had been at a meeting all morning and taking outpatient clinics all afternoon. Pete said he was expected any time now for a quick ward round. And Hannah's every pore ached to see Jon again.

At first she'd been disheartened that the kiss had not led to anything more. But on reflection, she had consoled herself — up to her ears in scented bubblebath and soaking till the bath water turned cold and the bangs on the door ever more persistent — what kiss could have been more thrilling? Better even than her dreams! You could hardly expect a proposal straight off. That would be taking fantasies to extremes, especially since Marcus had warned her Jon had this thing against marriage.

Let's take the campaign one step at a time, decided Hannah, bubbles foaming about her resolute chin. He likes me. He kissed me. But he wouldn't say he loves me. Perhaps he doesn't? Perhaps he does but he doesn't know he does. I've got to be patient because Marcus said so, but patience is not the greatest of my virtues. I'll have to make the most of my stubborn streak. I'm going to marry that man if it kills me!

As ever, a day on the wards had left little time to indulge in thoughts of self, let alone dreams of romance. Sometimes you were hard pressed to fit in a trip to the loo, let alone gulp down a bowl of soup and a cheese-and-lettuce roll. But since she was officially off duty

Hannah considered herself entitled to let her thoughts drift as she decorated the lofty windows with an aerosol of fake snow. She was attempting a seasonal Victorian copper-plate script, and it took a nice steady hand to get the flowing curves just right. 'A Merry Christmas'. The ward was enjoying a grandstand view of Nurse Westcott's shapely nether limbs all neat in black stockings.

'There! How does that look?'

There were always a number of men, neither too ill nor too elderly, ever-ready to appreciate their prettier nurses with loud and expressive comments. Hannah had long ceased to blush at their antics. 'Handy Hannah', she'd been nicknamed on the first men's ward she'd worked on, and at first she'd found it an ordeal just to walk the length of the long Nightingale wards under such lively scrutiny. If the female wards tended to be tidier and more determinedly attractive, male wards could be a lot of fun. Especially if Sister wasn't on duty.

But Jon might arrive at any moment. 'Shush,' she reproved them, biting her lip to conceal a smile, 'you mustn't say things like that or I'll get ticked off for supposedly encouraging you. Oops, I don't think this chair's safe at all.'

'I'll hold it for you, Nursie,' offered the PE teacher, Mr Symes, who was in for treatment of an over-active thyroid. 'I'd do the decorating, but we haven't started joined-up writing yet at my school.'

'Ho ho ho!' chorused his admiring captive audience, and it was into this riotous scene that Dr Harrington strode, with Pete Fuller loping two steps behind, raising questioning eyebrows as he realised Hannah was still there on the ward.

Smiling her thanks, Hannah sent her willing helper to his bed to be ready for the doctors' flying visit. She carried her chair along to the next window and took her time spraying an A fit to grace an illuminated manuscript. There was a washbasin not four feet distant and here Jon would stop to wash his hands between patients. The timbre of his deep voice was moving ever closer as he discussed treatments with his houseman. Hannah took a deep slow breath and tried to keep her hands from shaking over C-C-Christmas.

'Give him a litre of normal saline over the next half-hour.' Jon cleared his throat with a hhrrmph. Was he getting a cold? agonised Hannah. 'And could you get me a central venous pressure catheter kit — it's the only way to be sure we're giving the correct amount.' Hannah's anxious frown changed to a smile. How easy the two doctors sounded with each other now. Jon seemed of late more kindly disposed towards his young houseman.

Young! If Pete was twenty-six it was unlikely Jon was much older — five years perhaps? He just seemed so mature and impressive with his superior physical build and strength, his confident professional manner. As the French would say, *très formidable*. Formidable, dreamed Hannah, it was a wonderful, *perfect* word to describe darling Jon.

The footsteps were almost upon her. Hannah's heart gave a thrilling bound and she leaned over a bit more to show plenty of leg. Her spine prickled as she sensed the doctors were right behind her.

'Very impressive, Nurse,' murmured that mellow bass with such dry ambiguity that Hannah was at a loss to decide whether her legs or her artistry had earned her the compliment. 'But I fear your balancing act may raise some blood pressures around here. Wouldn't you agree, Dr Fuller?'

Pete dragged his eyes off Hannah's shapely calves and agreed enthusiastically. Hannah dropped her lashes and endeavoured to look modest rather than well pleased that Jon had noticed her legs were not her worst feature.

'Yes,' drawled Jon, 'that's a helluva drop out there. I should hate to think of you crashing through one of these windows.'

Tempted to aim the spray in Jon's direction, Hannah sprang down from her chair and looked the Registrar dead in the eye. 'Thank you, Dr Harrington, but I am being very careful.' She moved on ahead, but Jon's voice rang in her ears as she worked. They'd reached the bed of a young Welshman, Huw Davies, who only that afternoon had experienced one of his severest asthma attacks since he was admitted the previous week. Pete had been on the ward and dealt with the crisis so efficiently the other patients scarcely realised what had happened. To see another man fighting for breath in the throes of bronchial spasm was upsetting for them at the best of times.

'I gave Mr Davies 5mg of Salbutamol in the nebulizer, and reviewed him ten minutes later. The bronchial spasm responded well.'

Hannah couldn't hear the Registrar's response, but the tone sounded complimentary enough. He spent several minutes at Huw Davies' bedside and then the doctors moved on and out of earshot.

It was one of the few nights Hannah was not required at rehearsal. She washed her hair, just for something to do, wrote a letter home, tried to concentrate on *The Central Nervous System* and nursing management of related patient admissions, gave up and wandered off to see if Mango was back from her late night shopping. She admired the litter of purchases in their glitzy wrappings, and, against her better judgment, born of an inner bubbling joy that even common sense could not quench, bared her heart and soul before the fount of wisdom, knowing Mango would say, like Marcus, this love was Meant To Be.

Only Mango said nothing of the sort. And what she did say kept her friend awake half the night in an agony of hopelessness.

'I thought I'd better not mention that I'd seen Jon's brother at this party.'

'Why not? You know I'm well aware you two are 'old pals', as they say.' Hannah made no effort to conceal her hurt and surprise. 'It seems odd not to have mentioned it when you've known all along how I feel about Jon.'

'How your feelings have *changed* for Jon. Remember when you simply loathed him?'

In slow-motion denial Hannah shook her head. 'It doesn't seem possible now. I don't believe I ever did. It was a cover for emotions so strong they frightened me. He seemed so . . . so remote, so impossibly attractive.'

'Perhaps that's the right word for Dr Jonathan Boyd-Harrington,' said Mango harshly. 'Impossible. Can't you just forget him, Han, old thing? He's married to medicine. There's no place in his world for a wife, for children.'

'And how can you be so sure?' demanded Hannah indignantly, her pupils black with outrage, her heart thudding in her heaving breast. Maybe if one more person tells me, I might just get to believe it! 'And let me remind you the word 'impossible' is not in my vocabulary. Stubborn is my middle name.'

'Oh well,' shouted back Mango, 'if

you just want an affair then I dare say from the sound of it you're well on the way to starting one! Harrington's a cool customer. And he thinks you're one step removed from the nunnery, remember?'

The door flew wide and Home Sister was revealed in the full glory of her flowery quilted dressing-gown. 'What on earth is going on in here? It sounds like a bear garden! Nurse Westcott, get along to your bed.'

Hannah did as she was told, fuming that nurses, in spite of doing a job that required maturity and a readiness to shoulder responsibility, among all the other admirable qualities fundamental to the noble profession of nursing, should have to put up with being scolded like naughty children. Go to bed, Nurse, indeed! She put her slippers on and crept back along the corridor to Mango's room. 'There's something you haven't told me,' she accused her yawning friend. 'What are you keeping from me?'

'Switch the fire on,' groaned Mango. 'I can see I'll get no rest if I don't tell you. I was going to anyway, only you got in such a state and yelled the place down.'

The two of them huddled by the fire. 'If this is what being in love is all about,' muttered Hannah, 'I think I want out. I dreamed it'd all be romping through daisies and sharing bars of chocolate flake.'

'So it would be with men like Pete. But face up to it, Han, you've picked the wrong guy this time. Sebastian says Jon hasn't changed his mind, and he never will. Marriage is a disaster area. And he's no intention of repeating family history. He's told his mother — ' Here Mango hesitated, unsure if she should go on or if the truth would be just too cruel.

Hannah gripped her arm painfully. 'Go on,' she insisted, 'go *on*!'

The other girl avoided her urgent eyes, and shrugged. 'He's told her there'll never be any grandchildren, so she must save her hopes for Seb.'

I just don't understand it, Hannah

told herself, shaking her head in hurt and bemusement. That sounded pretty final. But it was all so hard to understand: Jon's lack of trust, his cool and aloof attitude towards human relationships. She, from the vantage point of a happy home and a caring family, trying to understand his point of view, and failing, totally failing.

'So you see,' Mango grasped and squeezed the stiff, chilled fingers, 'it would save so much hurt if you gave up on Jon. If even his brother believes he's a hopeless case — well, what's the use in breaking your heart, Hannie dear? There's plenty more fish in the sea.'

Hannah had taken all this much more reasonably than Mango had feared she would. She seemed a little pensive — which was understandable — but otherwise calm. The old Hannah might have reacted with more drama; tears and protests and avowals that her love and determination would win the day.

Poor old Han, yawned Mango as she

clambered back into her welcome bed. She's never had much luck in love. It's a terrible shame when she's a such a dear herself. But there's a dangerous quality about her that attracts the most unsuitable types, a kind of inner fire that singles her out from all the other pretty girls. All the same, I reckon that's my good deed for the day. Hearing the truth about Dr Harrington being a sworn bachelor has made Hannah see sense at long last.

11

'And now, ladies and gentlemen,' concluded the Prologue, a garrulous Dr Graeme Lewis from the Department of Pathology . . .

'Get on with it before we all die of boredom,' hooted a wag at the back of the auditorium, ' — *then* you'll have your work cut out!'

With impeccable dignity Dr Lewis ignored the interruption. 'Prepare your-selves for the theatrical experience of the year.' He waved his top hat and twiddled his false moustaches. 'Revel in this tale of the power of goodness to redeem misfortune. Shudder at the hideousness of the Beast. Mourn with our gorgeous heroine. Hiss at the two Evil Sisters and their *heartless* greed — '

'Chuck 'im off!' bawled the disre-spectful member of the audience. 'Give us an eyeful of Beauty!'

' . . . Sorrow with their merchant father, woo with the Seven Brothers, flirt with the Fairy . . . ' 'Oooooo!' came a chorus from the rear seats. 'I give you, one and all, our Christmas pantomime — *Beauty and her Beast*!' With a swirl of his silk cape, Dr Lewis was swallowed up in the swishing curtains and the orchestra took up where his voice left off as the high-kicking chorus-line, all lipstick and suspenders, came prancing gleefully on.

In the communal dressing room Hannah sat tight and waited for her first call, repeating her lines with heart a-thump and greasepaint making her eyelids itch and lips feel tacky with crimson gloss. 'Oh, my beloved Beast, I find happiness in the goodness I perceive deep within your heart. Many men are more monsters than you, their faces hiding . . . oh dear, oh dear, that's not right! . . . their faces concealing false, corrupt and *ungrateful* hearts. I care more for you than for such men. And yet, dear Beast, I cannot marry you.'

'Hannah! Hannah — you're on in two minutes!'

From the wings she could watch Pete and his Evil Sister coming to the end of their duet, all brash and brassy and beer-swilling; giving it everything they'd got as they roared out a paean to avarice — and the hope that Dad, the old fool, hadn't been and gone and forgotten the pearls and velvets and rich jewels he'd been nagged to bring back from his latest sea voyage to the East. And the red *rose* their stupid little sister had requested!

Grabbing her broom from the props table, Hannah was on stage before she knew it, singing with more tension than tenderness as she swept her kitchen, heaved fresh-baked loaves from the oven with her work-stained hands, then settled to polish the silver in honour of father's return. Gradually, the vice that had gripped her lungs at the first impact of lights and heat and the breathing darkness beyond relaxed its stranglehold and she sang more freely, earning herself the first of many bursts of enthusiastic applause, accompanied by whistles from the back of the auditorium.

Home came the unhappy merchant with the dire news of his bankruptcy and the ships lost in storms at sea. All he brought with him was the one red rose for Beauty.

'But, Father, it is winter! Where could you find such a flower?' Hannah relaxed and began to enjoy herself. Beauty was such an unreal heroine, all sweetness and light and an absolute pain, thought she, fluttering her eyelashes and clasping agitated hands. But the actress within was taking over the role and playing it right to the hilt. Hannah's eyes sparkled and her voice thrilled with its glorious silver tone. 'Pray, do not weep, dear Father. What does it matter if we are poor and have to move to a poor herdsman's cottage in Surrey?' . . . she paused as Marcus Shero had told her to, and the audience's groan came right on cue. A thrill of power rippled through her and she controlled the urge to join in the laughter.

Led to the Castle of the Beast by her sorrowing parent, Beauty is left to atone for his audacity in stealing the red rose from the Beast's magical garden. With downcast eyes she stares dumbstruck at the feet of the approaching dreadful creature to whom she must be sacrificed. Very slowly, Marcus had instructed, allow the head to lift and the eyes to register horror as they travel the length of this terrifying apparition . . . and reach his astonishing head.

Good grief! Hannah's jaw dropped and all her newfound spontaneity froze. This wasn't Gareth. This wasn't the leading man she'd been expecting! That mask and costume could only be concealing the six feet and four of one man. Dr Jonathan Harrington, her one and only Dr Beast . . . so where? so *why*? . . . so what in heaven's name was going on?

There and then the actress in Hannah fled. She dried. And it seemed

342

like an age before the muttered prompt from the wings set her in motion once again. Not that the audience noticed anything other than a highly realistic performance from the heroine, frozen to an icicle with incredulity at the apparition before her.

The Beast laid a hand upon her shoulder, leading her away to the room he had prepared specially for his exquisite captive. A curtain behind them lifted and they were in the bedchamber. 'Where's Gareth?' hissed Hannah as they presented their backs to the audience.

'Gone down with mumps. Caught it from his twin boys. You must swear,' the deep voice resounded in sombre, muffled tones, emerging through the rigid lips of the gruesome mask of the Beast, 'swear upon your father's life that you will stay here with me for three whole months.'

'I do swear,' uttered Hannah faintly. Then recalling where she was and what she was supposed to be doing, 'I do swear,' she repeated, injecting into her voice all the brave and pathetic dignity of poor captured Beauty, projecting her response to the back rows of the auditorium. Excitement suddenly gripped her. To be acting with Jon himself! The adrenalin surged and her eyes blazed with ardour. Just you try and get rid of me, Beast! they challenged with unspoken clarity. And the Beast's left eyebrow gave a quizzical, unscripted quirk.

'Your room is prepared for your coming. In yon magic mirror you will be able to see your father and your family as often as you wish. Where is your mother?'

'She is dead, sire, these twelve long years.'

'Ah!' Pause. Then, 'Do you find me repulsive, Beauty?'

Hannah pressed the back of her hand to her quivering lips. She nodded with a pretence of reluctance. 'I — I — do, sire.' The Beast turned sadly away, and on the impulse she fell to her knees and caught at his hand. 'But you are

very kind-hearted. My room is so lovely
. . . all these books, the piano.'

'Then if I ask you to marry me and
stay here with me for ever, shall you say
yes?'

'Oh, I cannot, I cannot!' Hannah threw
herself upon the floor, at the mercy of
her captor, in a sprawl of slithery pink
satin and a tumbling mass of shiny brown-
gold hair.

'Then every night I shall put to you
the same question. Every night I shall
ask you to marry me.'

The irony of it!

Hannah stood like a stone, her rueful
eyes upon the Beast as he limped away
into the wings. Her dream come true,
in front of an audience of hundreds. Yet
it was all pretence. She concealed the
wry twist of her vivid mouth, moving to
sit at the piano and accompany herself
in a melancholy ballad. And during the
burst of applause that followed, she
wandered wistfully across to her magic
mirror and as the curtain fell was
gazing sadly into its depths.

The stage hands hurried on to prepare the scene that Beauty was gazing upon — a riotous orgy of wine and song as the idle brothers and their women, and the evil, greedy sisters and their boyfriends, caroused while Father in his cold bedroom lay sick unto death in his miserable bed.

★ ★ ★

Iron wills are made to crack.

What's the use of breaking your heart over him, Hannie dear?

He'll *never* ask anyone to marry him!

Forget Jon Harrington. There's plenty more fish in the sea.

Hannah, I promise you, everything's going to work out just fine . . .

The Prince leaned low over the sleeping Beauty. 'I've given you your cue twice! Have you gone into a trance?'

Stumbling to her feet, toes catching in the long satin skirts of her Empire-line gown, Hannah pretended to rub sleepy eyes — taking care not to smear the dramatic artistry of her eye make-up. 'I must have been dreaming!' she exclaimed to an audience now so attentive you could have heard a pin drop. Her hand clutched at her throat as her eyes fell upon her transformed darling Beast.

The sight of Jon in Gareth's royal-purple tights was so alarming it brought on a fit of the giggles. You just dare! warned the Beast's all-seeing eye as Hannah's expressive face began to crumple. He towered above her, legs astride, fists on hips, a heavy velvet cloak lending dignity to clinging purple hose and doublet.

Hannah's eyes were simply popping. 'I was dreaming,' she recited mechanically, 'I still am.'

Jon could see the situation was deteriorating fast. Beauty was on the verge of hysteria: it had all been too much, the sudden change in her leading man — and these damn tights weren't meant for his sort of legs, how the hell Nureyev managed, he looked a biggish fellow . . . Jon hadn't had time to learn the next lines, but he was adept at thinking on his feet and he'd a fair idea of what came next. As for Beauty, she was in such a daze of confusion, poor kid, and who could blame her? Even if she sang like an angel, she was no professional actress.

Without batting an eyelid Jon came up with an adlibbed 'Oh no, you're not!' and the back rows spoke up for Hannah, with a chanted 'Oh yes, we are!' What a night this has turned out to be, marvelled the bemused heroine. May it never, never end.

And now for the most important bit of all, that would bring back life to the petrified Evil Sisters — turned into statues as punishment for their wicked ways; and demonstrate how Beauty's pity had turned to love.

The Kiss . . .

With an alacrity she'd never been able to muster when acting with Gareth, Hannah flung herself into the Beast's open arms and was quite literally swept off her feet as Jon caught her about the waist and swung her up till her head was on a level with his. In front of all these people! marvelled a scandalised Beauty, gazing helplessly into purple-grey eyes only inches from her own. If only an invisible cloak could be thrown over the two of them, so no one out there could see . . .

She retained just enough sensibility to realise her legs were dangling inelegantly, arranging her silver slippers in a pretty balletic pose and resting timid hands on the Beast's powerful shoulders. Well, Hannah! You're getting exactly what you wanted — but in the most embarrassingly public circumstances! Jon won't want to make too convincing a thing of it, though, the Kiss.

'Will you marry me *now*, dearest Beauty?' her Prince was asking in impassioned tones redolent of longing and hope. And taking her cue from this — for Hannah guessed she must be arm-achingly heavy even for Geoff Capes to hold aloft in such heroic fashion — she forgot her own lines of a dignified 'I will,' and cried hurriedly, 'Yes, yes, yes, my darling Beast!'

Next moment Jon's mouth was upon hers for real, not just acting — and she was being heartily kissed and the audience were going *mad* by the sound of it . . . Then with a secret wink Jon set her down on the dusty boards, the signal for the Evil Sisters to regain power of movement and join them centre stage. Out of the safety of Jon's arms Hannah felt awkwardly shy and embarrassed as with one hand in his and the other in her Evil Sister Pete's, with the rest of the cast grouped around them, one and all broke into the final chorus, swaying in their lines from side to side and urging the audience to join in with 'We Did It Our Way'.

The curtain calls went on and on . . . and on. Hannah's face began to ache with so much smiling. Nothing in the rest of her life was going to match the exhilaration of this moment, holding Jon's hand for all the world to see: the cheers he got as he strode forward to take his solo bow almost raised the roof, for everyone realised now that he'd stepped in to give a remarkable performance and fill the breach.

For her final scene Hannah had a change of costume and hairdo: a magnificent romantic crinoline in sky-blue silk, its tightly laced bodice cut low-and-behold and trimmed with lace and rose-coloured satin ribbons. An elaborate ringleted white wig, Marie-Antoinette style, to complete her outfit. And the whistles and catcalls which greeted her solo curtsey when Jon pushed her to the front of the stage brought a blush to her cheeks that wouldn't have disgraced a field full of swaying poppies.

At the first opportunity Hannah slipped out to merge with the audience and seek out Helen and Bram. The whole cast was sky-high on adrenalin, surging down to greet their friends in full costume before the party celebrations got under way.

There was Helen, a sumptuous creamy fur jacket about her shoulders, real pearls in her ears and at her white neck. And Bram — gorgeous Bram, gathering a sister in each arm and kissing Hannah's glowing cheek as she clutched at his jacket front. 'Was I all right? Did you enjoy the show? Helen, was your seat comfortable — is your back hurting?'

Their praises were music in her ears. But Hannah really wanted to talk about Jon's performance. 'What did you think of him? Wasn't he incredibly marvellous, stepping in at the last moment and saving the show? I'd absolutely no idea. Did you notice that? Absolutely stunned . . . '

Helen couldn't resist the whispered teasing reminder that she supposed the part was tailor-made for Hannah's Dr Beast, and Hannah had the grace to look crestfallen and sorry for all the misunderstandings of the past. 'Come to the party,' she urged, 'and I'll introduce you. Think how my stock will soar when people see me in the company of the eminent surgeon, Mr Bram Markland!'

Bram came down from the lofty heights to give his young sister-in-law a swift, warm embrace. 'Helen's not much of a night bird just at the moment. I must take her home to her bed.' As Hannah's face fell he squeezed her hand. 'You do understand — she's so precious to me, I have to wrap her up in cotton wool.'

Hannah pulled herself together and forced gaiety into her voice; if Jon had been able to see her with so important a man as Bram, then he might have a better opinion of her. 'Looks more like wrapping her in mink to me!' she joked, stroking the lustrous fur.

'We must go, dear. And someone's busting a gut over there trying to attract your attention — Mango, hello!'

Pushing her way towards Mango through the noisy throng, Hannah was showered from all sides with compliments. Hands caught at the silvery ringlets spilling over her right shoulder and clustering at the nape of her neck, stroked the gorgeous fabric of her costume, borrowed for the occasion from the wardrobe of the National.

Mango's hand closed warningly over her friend's wrist. 'Steel yourself for a shock, kid. Look who's here and demanding to speak to you ... Hannah, you remember meeting Sebastian Boyd-Harrington on that holiday in France?'

'And I dare say you won't quite have forgotten *me*.'

So many hours foolishly wasted in sleeplessness, imagining how she'd cope with the shock if she should ever come face to face with Dr Richard Derby again. She might blanch, tremble; her heart might even stop. And in reality I feel ... nothing! Hannah realised, but with no particular satisfaction. You're a curiosity now, Dickie, from my past. Yes, I feel a stirring of interest at seeing how you've changed ... not much, though, nothing to speak of. And from your eyes I can see you wouldn't mind picking up where we left off. Only *I'm* the one who's changed. I'm not the Hannah Westcott you twisted round your little finger. And someone else now has the power to stop the beat of my heart and keep me wakeful half the night.

'How lovely to see you again, Sebastian,' she exclaimed warmly. 'And you too, Dickie,' she added politely, accepting their congratulations with poise and asking what they were doing with themselves these days.

'We're both working in Birmingham — SHOs on surgical firms. You two should come up and visit us one of these days. Show you the sights. Could be good getting to know each other again, eh, Hannah?' Dickie was wary of her. Attracted, she could see that reflected in his eyes as they lingered on the black beauty-patches the make-up department had stuck high on her cheekbone and low on the creamy flesh displayed above the frilled neckline. Oh yes, tonight she was artificially beautiful and sophisticated, a manufactured object of desire. And Dickie was fascinated by the change in her. It was only fair to put him straight.

She looked him directly in the eye. 'I really couldn't care if I never see you again,' she said simply. It wasn't intended to hurt, indeed Derby had the hide of a rhinoceros; but in front of Sebastian it rather spoiled his Lothario image.

'Of course there's bound to be someone else by now, I realise that,' he said hurriedly to save his own reputation from outright rejection, while Sebastian guffawed into his beer mug and Mango nudged Dickie in the ribs.

'She's a big girl now,' she informed the two doctors, 'and she's got a real man in her life . . . not that I'm going to tell you who!'

'This is a very interesting conversation,' observed a deep well of a voice. 'Can anyone join in?' The sudden warmth of the hand on her nipped-in waist, accompanying this verbal interruption, took Hannah so by surprise that she cried out in shock far greater than Dr Derby had been able to conjure. 'How are you, brother mine?' enquired Jon Harrington. 'I take it no news is good news.'

While Jon and Sebastian talked medical shop Jon's hand stayed firmly where it was, in proprietorial possession of Hannah. Dickie's mouth was grim as he put two and two together and came up with some answers he clearly found totally improbable. Jon and Hannah? Never. But why not? The kid was a woman now, that was clear. And who better fitted the description 'real man' than the macho Dr Harrington himself? Why ever hadn't Seb warned him . . .

Dickie tried unsuccessfully to determine what was going on from Mango, but she just shrugged and rolled those huge black eyes of hers and clearly intended to give nothing away. It was Seb who dropped the bombshell into their midst.

'Nigel's putting it about that Camilla's going to announce her engagement at long last. Is that true, Jon?'

'I believe I can safely say she is.'

'I hope,' asserted the younger brother, 'that Camilla is indebted to you for your splendid cover job. The press were certainly caught on the hop!'

Hannah dared not speak. Jon was standing so close against her that the whole of her left side seemed on fire with raw nerve ends. When Jon spoke she could feel the timbre of his voice reverberate right through her. 'Quite indebted,' he agreed mockingly. If he was upset by losing Camilla then he must be a consummate actor — or so adept at maintaining his cool control that emotion never moved from the confines of his brain. Either, mused Hannah despondently, was a likely facet of this clever, compelling hunk of man.

'Who is he?' demanded Mango, expressing the curiosity of all.

'Why,' admitted Jon, 'the American tennis star, Bruce Dalniell.'

Mango exploded. 'Lord! They'll be absolutely mobbed when the paparazzi get hold of this! I reckon you're a real Boy Scout, Dr Harrington! I hope they ask you to be best man.'

Sebastian aimed a playful punch at his brother's even loftier shoulder. 'Now you're free to find yourself a best woman, eh? Bring tears of joy to Mother's eyes at long last. Hannah looks pretty handy for starters, eh? A pretty nurse on the arm is worth a bedfull of brainless beauties . . . '

Quivering with mortification, Hannah wrenched herself out of Jon's amused grasp. She muttered something about the wig making her head ache, and fled the party with all the desperate haste of Cinderella on the stroke of midnight, skirts gathered high as she rushed out of the medical school building and back to where they'd changed and been made up and where her own safe Hannah-clothes were waiting. It had been a lot of fun, playing Beauty; so much excitement, and the thrill of being made much of for a couple of evenings in your life. There would be other pantomimes. But there'd never be anyone who would mean as much to her as Jon. And to be teased was more than she could bear — even if Seb hadn't realised how close to the truth he was probing; even if he hadn't meant to rub it in that his brother was so determinedly not the marrying kind.

'You're sick, Dr Harrington, if you think marriage is some kind of trap that changes people's personalities as soon as they're legally bound to one another. I love you — and nothing can change that. Nothing will change that. Whether I see you again or not, I shall always love you. But if ever *we* should meet unexpectedly in the future, as Dickie and I have done today, I don't know how I should bear it.'

With rapid, jerky movements Hannah fixed her hair back with a length of crepe bandage and smeared vanishing cream all over her face and neck. 'It's a form of illness, Doctor! And we treat all forms of illness, don't we, on Grenville. With tests, tests and more tests. There must be a test I can think of to show my diagnosis is right! You're going to love me back, Dr Harrington, if I have to mix you a magic potion.'

Hannah's mind was in a fever of emotion as she sought out ways to make herself more lovable to Jon. Wouldn't you think that in the twentieth century, with all its miracle drugs, there'd be something in that special locked medicine cupboard on Grenville to make Jon see the light?

Back in her room Hannah fumbled beneath her mattress for the secret diary she'd been keeping. The log of where and when she saw Jon, what had happened, what they had said with their eyes as much as with words and gestures. For twenty minutes she wrote solidly, then she laid down her pen and, sighing, flicked the pages back to the empty spaces of her life before, for her, Dr Harrington existed. The story of Hannah Westcott. Twenty-one next February. She buried her head in inky hands. *Madness* to imagine a man of Jon's years and experience could take a serious interest in a girl of only twenty-one.

But there was *one* medicine she could try. Hannah's hands fled to her mouth. Her hazel eyes fastened upon some unseen point in the future. It *could* work. But only in very special circumstances when Jon would be at his most magnanimous and at peace with the world. The timing was crucial. But if you happened to be sufficiently desperate, if it meant so much, if the man was worth risking your career for . . .

Hannah shivered. If this didn't work out, the treatment would backfire. She would be the one to be grievously hurt. No danger whatsoever for Dr Harrington; he'd just carry on in his determined way; after wiping the floor with her, of course. Wed as always to medicine alone.

When over an hour later her door opened stealthily and Mango's voice whispered, 'Han — are you awake?' she feigned the deepest of sleep. Confiding in Mango was right out now: this must be carried out alone. Two days free to plan the campaign down to the last move. And then a week to select the vital moment.

To win — or to lose — Dr Harrington's impervious heart.

12

'Merry Christmas, Sister French, and all . . . ' declaimed Pete Fuller, with the convivial lack of co-ordination of one who'd been offered 'a drop of sherry, Doctor?' on every ward he'd visited that Christmas Eve.

'And to you, Dr Fuller.' Sister surveyed the tottering heap of chocolate boxes piled high on her office desk. 'Now why don't I retire and start a sweet shop?'

'Take some home for all your kiddies,' advised Pete. 'If Hannah stuffs any more, we'll never get her out through the ward doors.'

'Shouldn't dream of it. Such generosity from our patients is meant for the staff to enjoy.' Sister locked the filing cabinet and handed her staff nurse two bunches of keys. 'All yours now, Bea. And the best of luck. I'm off home to peel sprouts and fill stockings. Twelve tomorrow for roast turkey and all the trimmings. No peace for the wicked!'

'Oh, my goodness,' murmured Hannah faintly, her head swimming on one small sherry. Excitement and trepidation were creating havoc with her insides, and she hadn't eaten a proper meal all day — just the chocs pressed upon her by those men remaining on the ward for treatment. It was the tension — Christmas coming upon them all so fast . . . And the way she was planning to celebrate it. One wild indulgent fling.

Sister, seeing how the young nurse was chewing the inside of her cheek, hazel eyes glazed with longing, assumed it was wishful thinking fighting with Hannah's natural good manners. 'Take no notice of him, dear,' she comforted, pushing an opened box of Milk Tray into Hannah's hands. 'You're thin as a lath, you lucky girl. Eat all you want.' She allowed Pete to help arrange her cloak gallantly about her shoulders and took the shopping basket he had rescued from behind the filing cabinet.

'Well, Doctor,' she said, her brown eyes crinkling as she lifted her head to smile up at Pete, 'we shall be losing you soon, as well as our two second-years. All of you moving on and upward.'

'But you'll still see me about the place — scalpel flashing between me teeth and scrubbed to the eyebrows. It'll suit my temperament better, don't you think, surgery?' He grabbed the Milk Tray from Hannah and put on a wild-eyed stance as if poised to embark on some dangerous mission. 'They *must* be delivered!'

Bea snatched the box back. 'Heaven help Mr O'Sullivan with you on his firm! And what's behind the gossip I've been hearing about you and that young staff nurse who's got her first Sister's post? What's her name, I forget . . . '

Pete glanced guiltily at Hannah, half hoping to catch her looking stricken. But her eyes smiled encouragement, for the last thing she could have borne was the thought of that sparky temperament

366

getting a dampening on her account. He cheered up on the instant. He'd never get anywhere with Hannah; not seriously. She was a puzzle all right. A terrific girl. But whatever it was she'd set her sights on, Pete Fuller knew he didn't figure in Hannah's plans. And Suzy Wycliffe was proving extremely pleasant consolation.

★ ★ ★

It was Hannah's first experience of Christmas Day on the wards. Only the ill patients remained, those who were ambulant having been allowed home just for the holiday. The atmosphere on Grenville was, however, far from melancholy. Bright-eyed children trooped round the hospital singing carols. Duty doctors wandered amiably in and out. The usual ebb and flow of physios and social workers and dietitians had trickled to the minimum needed to maintain the services over the holiday.

Dr Harrington arrived with the chaplain, Father Richardson, who gave the Christmas blessing to all and said Grace over a steaming golden turkey. For Hannah it was a reminder of times past, when, little more than toddlers, with her two sisters she'd been led on Christmas Day round the wards of Dad's local hospital, clutching on to the skirts of his black cassock as he too blessed the sick and carved the first slice of the turkey. Watching the nurses in awe and envy of their crisp uniforms and calm authoritative airs.

This was a day when no one wanted to admit to feeling ill; but when those who were very poorly got lots of extra TLC from the nurses, who had more time than usual to sit and chat at bedsides.

Jon was demonstrating impeccable surgical skills as he reduced a huge and juicy bird to meticulous slices, guaranteed to tempt the most jaded appetite. He even sported a purple paper crown to match his eyes of thunder-grey — though stormy weather was very far from everyone's thoughts as the Senior Registrar with endless bonhomie kept up a stream of jocularity with patients and nurses alike.

'And a morsel for Nurse Westcott,' he called, holding aloft within his fingers a succulent sliver of white meat for Hannah's lips.

'Is this my medicine, sir,' she had the wit and presence of mind to respond — while marvelling inside at her own coolness — 'or part of my calorie-controlled diet?'

'No diets for you — I like you exactly as you are,' muttered Jon close to her ear as she leaned over the trolley to spoon glistening buttery sprouts on to a plate. The plate in her outstretched hand wobbled so evidently that Jon, intrigued, added teasingly in a low intimate murmur: 'Every perfect inch . . . ' He was, he acknowledged it himself, a little the worse for wear, having been toasted on every ward he'd visited since breakfast. And Nurse Westcott's blushing confusion was arousing within him the most unsuitable ideas, considering they were both still strictly on duty. He simply couldn't take his eyes off her; and it seemed the feeling was mutual if he was any judge of those beautifully sparkling hazel eyes.

Jon's mouth tightened as he considered the facts. All these years he'd been so sure of what he wanted. And what he did not! And while no one enjoyed the company of women more than he, his upbringing had convinced him he must stay free of ties. Concentrate solely on a profession too vital to be subject to compromise. But lately, thanks to the fireworks sparked off by a certain young woman, Jon had found himself in the most peculiar situation, his sureness undermined and his philosophies threatened. He'd have sworn he was, at thirty-two, too old to change. But Hannah had taught him in her irresistible fashion — for it was clear to Jon that she was in love with him, but that for her nothing less than marriage would do — that while he could not alter his upbringing, he could certainly change his outlook. And recently Jon had discovered he was fighting a losing battle against this Joan of

Arc who'd made him dwell with pleasure on thoughts of children of his own, a home, and . . . yes, he admitted it, a wife.

Well, mused Jon, watching Hannah beneath speculative heavy lids, who could tell what the New Year might bring?

'There's a brandy waiting for you in the office, sir,' said Staff Phillips, 'if you'd like one before you go. Sister left a bottle in the filing cabinet.'

'If you'll have one with me, Staff,' said Jon, leading the way ahead.

Hannah idled the next five minutes away in the treatment room, trying to calm herself with breathing exercises which didn't seem to be having the least effect on her racing pulses and trembling limbs. Now or never . . . and there was Jon wishing Bea a Merry Christmas and his footsteps heading towards her and the swing doors.

Now! Hannah's fingers closed over the delicate berried sprig in her pocket. I can't do this, her insides screamed.

You've darn well got to, prodded her stubborn core. It's treatment time for Dr Harrington.

Too late! He'd passed the door. It galvanised Hannah into action. 'Jon!'

He heard the desperation in her call and hesitated, puzzled to see Hannah, ashen-faced, begging him with her huge dark-lashed eyes to turn back. A strange calm came over her when he was there in the flesh not three feet distant. 'Close the door,' she said, and quite forgot about the please, he was so much too good for her and so much more even than she remembered.

'*Your* medicine, Dr Jon,' she said softly, taking her hand out of her pocket.

'You want me to eat that?' protested Jon good-humouredly, taking the little sprig of berries in his hand and examining it before lifting it slowly to his mouth, as if he really were . . .

Gently Hannah stayed his hand.

'Don't you know how expensive mistletoe medicine is? It isn't available on the NHS — '

'Or listed in MIMS.'

'And of course it's a deadly poison when administered orally.'

'Quite,' agreed Jon solemnly, grasping the gist of Hannah's proposed 'treatment' with commendable intelligence and foresight.

'It's more of a test — like with litmus paper,' explained Hannah, her fingers still reining in the hand with which Jon had made to swallow his medicine, while his right arm coiled inescapably about her.

As he bent towards her, that lock of hair slipped over his brow and Hannah found herself thinking it gave Jon a wicked raffish air that she would enjoy getting accustomed to even more intimately. 'You mean,' he was whispering, lips pressed against her throbbing temple, 'that what I have to do is hold the mistletoe over our heads, while we . . . '

'That's right,' murmured Hannah, nestling against his white coat, and slipping her arms round the body inside. Five minutes later Jon said, 'Oh dear, I'm afraid I dropped the berries — and we've trodden on them. Did I — um — pass the test?'

'Oh, I was the one being tested, Dr Harrington. How do you think *I* did?'

Never relaxing the determination of his hold, and thinking to himself that if it wasn't Christmas and he hadn't been drinking brandy and if it was anyone but Hannah Westcott, he'd be regretting this moment for the rest of his life, Jon tilted a finger beneath that stubborn Westcott chin. 'May I tell you, Nurse, that right from the moment I first clapped eyes on you, I discovered you were likely to pass every test in my book with flying colours?'

Hannah's eyes filled with unstoppable tears. 'That's the nicest thing anyone's ever said to me. And yet you told Dickie Derby I was totally unsuitable for a doctor's wife!'

'*You* were far too good for *him*. I'd never liked what I heard from Seb about Richard Derby. Not that I expected our paths ever to cross again. If I'd had any idea you might overhear and misunderstand my intention I should have restrained myself, of course, from interfering. Let me tell you, I was mighty astonished when you turned out to be my model for that physiology demo. And I was baffled by the way you glared at me with those beautiful eyes and obviously shuddered every time I touched you.'

'You haven't exactly encouraged *me* either!' exclaimed Hannah. 'Here I've been, eating my heart out for even the hint of a smile — '

'And dating one of my own house-men too,' Jon chided gently. 'At first I took you for a serious-minded girl who ought to be allowed to get on with her training, undisrupted by lovesick Registrars. I believed that if I waited till then, concealing my true feelings . . . but every time I came on the ward I caught you and Pete Fuller fooling about like a couple of adolescents. I tell you, I didn't know what to make of you. Especially when I discovered you were considered of high academic calibre and could have read medicine yourself if you'd wanted.'

'Oh, *that*,' protested Hannah, shamefacedly fiddling with Jon's lapels.

'So,' murmured the doctor, quizzically examining the averted profile with its pouting mouth and heavy-lashed lids, 'does Nurse Westcott consider she can handle a love affair with me *and* carry on working for state finals at one and the same time?'

There was only one answer to that. But — a love affair! Was that all Jon had in mind? A temporary relationship leading to nowhere?

Hannah pulled away from Jon and put the space of the treatment room between them.

She squeezed her eyes tight shut and said very rapidly, 'Dr Harrington, will-you-marry-me?' then waited for the terse exclamation she was going to have to plead against. Six whole days of the Leap Year left — to wear Jon down with repeat after repeat after repeat. Or face a four-year wait till the next chance.

Silence. Perhaps he hadn't understood her gabbled question. Hannah put it again. 'Jon — will you marry me? *Will* you marry me, Jon?' Pride was of no consequence at a time like this. She dared to open an eye and squint doubtfully at the tall dark man opposite, his mouth and chin covered by a very dismayed hand.

'Look, Jon.' Hannah's eyes were huge and green and ardent. 'I do understand about you hating marriage. But you're not going through life all on your own — not if I can prevent it. And no one could ever possibly love you *half* as much as I do!'

'Forgive me,' said Jon, his voice muffled behind his hand, 'but it is a bit confusing. I mean to say, not so long ago you most vehemently insisted I was the most hateful man in the world. Now you want to marry me! Is it that you feel sorry for me? That I'm to be one of your lame ducks, as it were?'

A slow suspicion was by now suggesting itself to Hannah, that inadvertently she had stumbled upon the magic formula that would bring a smile to the face of Dr Jon. Behind his hand he was laughing at her! In a rustle of starched skirts she was across that room and grabbing his concealing hand. 'I thought so! You *are* laughing at me. Really, Jon, you are a beast! I'd like to know just what's so funny about being proposed to? I should have thought that considering this phobia you're suffering from, this distrust of marriage, you'd be halfway down that corridor by now instead of grinning your head off.'

'That's your diagnosis, is it?' His hands encircled each skinny wrist, holding her fast. 'I have a . . . phobia!'

The capped head bobbed vigorously. 'But phobias can be overcome. Even if everyone seems convinced you're married to medicine.' Pinioned against an expanse of palest blue poplin, Hannah was achingly aware of that other heart thundering away ominously above her own. How it spurred her on in the certainty of her conviction! Heartbeats spoke louder than words. Either that — or Jon needed to consult a specialist about his blood pressure. 'Since I recently discovered it was Leap Year I decided I should pop the question myself. I really don't see why that has to be a male prerogative. So what's your answer going to be, Jon? Are you going to marry me?'

'Of course I'm going to marry you! In all my thirty-two years you're the only woman I've ever considered spending the rest of my life with.' There was a new and tender wonder in his voice, as if even Jon was surprised to hear himself admitting he had feelings just like any other man. 'But *I* had intended to wait till you passed your state finals, Miss Westcott. Trust you not to have the patience to contain yourself. I suppose you'd like to be a spring bride — if we can persuade Miss Johnson to allow you an Easter holiday.'

'Oh, gosh!' breathed Hannah, 'I do

think you'd better come home next week and meet my family. Mmmmm . . . '

Bea Phillips opened the door none too quietly — and stopped short on the threshold. The entwined couple carried on oblivious, on the floor by their feet a few crushed white berries and a leafy green sprig. Bea's smile was as huge as a slice of watermelon. With stealthy care she closed the door and tiptoed back to the main ward: on Grenville they had a cure for everything.

THE END

Other titles in the
Linford Romance Library:

HUSHED WORDS

Angela Britnell

Cassie, a struggling single mother, and Jay, a wealthy financier, share a holiday romance in Italy; when fate throws them together again their sizzling passion rekindles. Cassie's family problems combined with Jay's fear of commitment and growing dissatisfaction with his lifestyle make their idea of a future together a dream. Jay can't ask for a second chance with Cassie until he discovers a new direction in life and lays it all on the line with the woman he loves.

TRUST IN ME

Rena George

When Kerra Morrison is named main beneficiary in her uncle's will, her cousins Sarah and David are furious their father favoured her over them. So when someone attempts to sabotage Kerra's new tearoom, her cousins seem to be the obvious culprits. But are there darker forces at work? The town's GP, Dr Duncan Crombie, comes to her aid. It would be easy to fall for such a man — if he didn't keep throwing up barriers every time they seem to be getting close . . .

DANGEROUS AFFAIR

Irena Nieslony

Feisty Eve Masters has had enough of the rat race. A successful career in London has allowed her to retire at forty-three and move to Crete. There, she falls for the handsome, but quiet, David Baker — but despite the mutual attraction, theirs is a volatile relationship. However, this is not the only thing to keep Eve occupied. The day she arrives, an English ex-pat estate agent is found murdered. Eve is intent on solving the crime — putting her own life in danger . . .

THE HEART IS TORN

Phyllis Mallett

Cornwall, 1782. Beth Farrell, betrothed to Adam Traherne, awaits his return from the Americas — but she fears his ship is lost. And trouble is now looming at home. Her father has drunk and gambled away his fortune, and fallen prey to the unscrupulous Jonah Peake, who desires Beth. Caught in a web of deceit and intrigue, Beth wonders if she will ever find happiness with the man she truly loves.

BONFIRE MEMORIES

Sally Quilford

Guy Sullivan's arrival in the quiet village of Midchester ruffles feathers and stirs up old memories, not least for Cara Baker, who had all but forgotten a frightening incident from her childhood . . . As she helps Guy find out what happened to his sister, she begins to fall in love. But she's made mistakes in the past, and with a murderer on the loose setting the village alight, Cara might get her fingers burned in more ways than one.